SO-BFG-157

# She moistened her lips nervously as she looked up into his eyes

She was shocked by the surge of desire that had sprung to life so easily. She wanted him to kiss her. She felt her heart thudding hard and painfully against her ribs. Feeling totally at a loss as to what to say or do, she did nothing, just looked up at him, waiting.

**KATHRYN ROSS** was born in Zambia where her parents happened to live at that time. Educated in Ireland and England, she now lives in a village near Blackpool, Lancashire. Kathryn is a professional beauty therapist, but writing is her first love. As a child she wrote adventure stories and at thirteen was editor of her school magazine. Happily, ten writing years later, she sold her first romance to Harlequin® Books. A romantic Sagittarian, she loves traveling to exotic locations.

# Kathryn Ross

# BRIDE BY DECEPTION

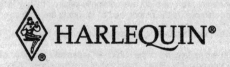

TORONTO • NEW YORK • LONDON
AMSTERDAM • PARIS • SYDNEY • HAMBURG
STOCKHOLM • ATHENS • TOKYO • MILAN • MADRID
PRAGUE • WARSAW • BUDAPEST • AUCKLAND

If you purchased this book without a cover you should be aware
that this book is stolen property. It was reported as "unsold and
destroyed" to the publisher, and neither the author nor the
publisher has received any payment for this "stripped book."

ISBN 0-373-18815-3

BRIDE BY DECEPTION

First North American Publication 2003.

Copyright © 2000 by Kathryn Ross.

All rights reserved. Except for use in any review, the reproduction or
utilization of this work in whole or in part in any form by any electronic,
mechanical or other means, now known or hereafter invented, including
xerography, photocopying and recording, or in any information storage
or retrieval system, is forbidden without the written permission of the
publisher, Harlequin Enterprises Limited, 225 Duncan Mill Road,
Don Mills, Ontario, Canada M3B 3K9.

All characters in this book have no existence outside the imagination of
the author and have no relation whatsoever to anyone bearing the same
name or names. They are not even distantly inspired by any individual
known or unknown to the author, and all incidents are pure invention.

This edition published by arrangement with Harlequin Books S.A.

® and TM are trademarks of the publisher. Trademarks indicated with
® are registered in the United States Patent and Trademark Office, the
Canadian Trade Marks Office and in other countries.

Visit us at www.eHarlequin.com

**Printed in U.S.A.**

# CHAPTER ONE

CALLUM tried not to let his eyes wander towards the clock in the elegant hotel lounge, but he was aware that he was leaving it late to catch his train.

'So, Francis, are you going to sign the contract or not?' He kept his tone jovial, no hint of his impatience.

The man looked up. Despite the lines of age on his face, the periwinkle-blue eyes were sharp and assessing. 'Sure, you're not in a hurry now are you, Callum?' he asked in his lilting Irish accent. 'I'd like to read over the small print one more time.'

'Well, if you want to.' Callum shrugged. There was a lot of money at stake here. He supposed he could catch the next train.

Francis gave a satisfied smile and caught the waitress's attention. 'Could we have another pot of tea, please?'

'Certainly, sir.' The waitress gave a smile at Callum, her eyes flicking admiringly over his dark hair and powerfully handsome physique, before hurrying away.

'Can't do business without a strong pot of tea.' Francis smiled and returned his attention to the papers.

Callum restrained himself from tapping his fingers on the table. This was their third pot of tea. What the hell was Francis Bernard playing at? The deal was no different than the one he had signed last year. He suppressed a sigh. Bernards was one of the largest chains of supermarkets. The farm needed this lucrative contract so he'd just have to exercise his patience.

Francis watched the waitress pour their tea. She was blonde and very attractive. She kept smiling at Callum but,

5

apart from a polite thank you, Callum Langston seemed unaware of the power of his looks.

'So, how are things on that farm of yours?' Francis asked suddenly, putting the contract to one side.

'Fine…ticking along, you know how it is.'

'And you're still on your own up there?'

Callum frowned. 'Hardly on my own, Francis. I've got two children as you know.'

'I meant, you haven't remarried?'

Callum shook his head.

Francis looked concerned. 'It can't be easy with no one to help you run that big rambling estate, and two young children to look after as well.'

'I've got a housekeeper.'

'Full-time is she?'

'Well, no, part-time actually.' Callum frowned.

'So, you could be doing with someone else?'

'Things are OK the way they are. Since my wife died, my mother helps out a lot.' Thinking about Ellen made Callum's gaze wander towards the clock. His train was due to leave Euston in just under an hour. If he caught it, he could collect the children from school and save Ellen the trip. She had looked tired recently.

'That's a pity.' Francis sat forward on his chair. 'Because if you were willing to take on someone else, someone I could recommend to you, I'd double the figure we're talking about on this contract.' He tapped the papers in front of him.

He had Callum's full attention now. 'What's this about, Francis?'

Francis paused. 'It's my daughter.' He said the words heavily as if they weighed a ton on his lips. 'I'm looking to settle her down.'

Callum's dark eyebrows shot up, then his lips twitched in amusement. 'This conversation isn't for real is it? Settle her down? You do realise this is the twenty-first century, don't you, Francis?'

'I don't want to play the heavy-handed father, Callum. But Zoë has always been a rebel. She's twenty-three, my only child, and she's breaking my heart.'

'I'm sorry to hear that. But I don't see what it has to do with me—'

'I need to get her out of London,' Francis cut across him abruptly. 'Just for a few weeks. I was hoping you might help.'

'You have my sympathy, Frank. But I don't see how I can help. And I really don't want to be caught in the cross-fire of family problems. Besides, I'm happy with our contract the way it is.'

'Well, perhaps I'll have to think some more about our contract. Maybe you could give me a bit longer; my accountants will have to look at it. I'll need a few days…or a few weeks.'

'Oh, come on, Frank. It's the same contract as last year. What is this? Blackmail?'

'Certainly not!' Francis looked at him reproachfully. 'All I'm saying is, you scratch my back, and I'll scratch yours.'

Callum pursed his lips and studied the man opposite. They'd met a few years ago at a conference on organic farming and, despite the difference in their age and backgrounds, they had hit it off. They'd talked long and hard about the pros and cons of modern farming and the retail world. And, after that, the orders had poured in for Callum, and it had helped turn the farm around.

He supposed he owed the guy quite a lot, Callum reflected. He also admired and respected him. Francis was a self-made millionaire who still retained control of his empire and tried to run it with the same, hands-on approach with which he had run his corner stores. Callum had always known he was eccentric, but this…this was plain ridiculous. 'Why would the daughter of a millionaire want to come and work as a housekeeper on a farm out in the middle of nowhere?'

'She doesn't know she wants to do that…yet. She'll never admit it to me but I recognise she's searching for something in her life…something real and solid. Something more meaningful than the shallow round of parties and socialising she has at the moment.'

Callum's lips twisted in sardonic amusement. 'She'd rather be out in the bleak mid-winter of the Cumbrian hills than sailing around the Caribbean?'

Francis nodded. 'She's done the Caribbean a lot.'

'Is she on drugs or something?' Callum's eyes narrowed. 'You're not using my farm as a rehab centre, Frank. I don't care how much money—'

'No…nothing like that. Though I do admit, I have reasons for wanting her out of London. To be specific, she's got caught up with the wrong man.'

'I see.' Callum shook his head. 'Well, count me out, Frank. I'm sorry, but this is way out of my depth. I think your daughter is entitled to see who she wants—'

'Matthew Devine is a small-time crook and a confidence trickster—'

'And your daughter is a twenty-three-year-old woman. Old enough to be able to run her life and make her own mistakes.'

'OK, I'll treble the offer on our contract,' Frank said without hesitation.

Callum felt a tremor of weakness enter his firm resolve. He really could use the money. He had men to employ, and the farm had been struggling recently.

'Why would the daughter of a millionaire, a woman who sails off to the Caribbean at a moment's notice, come to Cumbria as a housemaid?' he asked again.

'She's going through one of her rebellious phases again.'

Francis frowned. 'It's nothing unusual. Won't live in the apartment I bought her, won't take the job I organised for her. And, as a final act of defiance, she's taken to working for a recruitment agency. They send her out on odd jobs, short-term contracts. She covers for people who are ill or on maternity leave, that kind of thing. Won't last long.'

'How do you know?'

'I told you, she's in one of her rebellious moods.' Francis waved a hand. 'She's working as a chef now at a restaurant in Oxford Circus. I suppose that's thanks to the fancy finishing school I sent her to in Switzerland although, God knows, at the time I didn't think it would lead her to the kitchens of London. I had much higher hopes than that for her. Before that, she was playing housekeeper to a rock star in Chelsea. She plays these games, then she gets bored, comes back, and I offer to increase her allowance again so that she can jet off on another holiday.'

Sounded like a spoilt brat, Callum thought with distaste.

'Only, this time, it's different. This time I don't think she's going to come back. Well, not until she's played the ultimate game, marrying Mr Totally Unsuitable. Then I'm really going to have a mess on my hands.'

'I'd let her get on with it,' Callum said firmly.

'Maybe you would.' Francis shrugged. 'But she's my only child and I love her. Also…Callum, I wasn't going to tell you this…' Francis sighed suddenly '…but, I've only discovered recently, that I haven't got long to sort this out…'

'How do you mean?' Callum frowned.

'In blunt terms, I'm not a well man. Can you imagine how it feels to know that I might leave my daughter in the merciless clutches of a man like Matthew Devine?' Francis leaned forward anxiously. 'The thought of it is more than flesh and blood can stand. I'm appealing to you, Callum, not just as a business associate, but also as a friend, and one father to another. Please help me deal with this situation.'

Callum stared at him, genuinely shocked by his news. The poor man wasn't old. He could only be sixty-two, maybe sixty-five at most. 'I sympathise, Francis.'

Francis nodded and reached to sip his tea. 'But will you help?'

'If your daughter is so caught up with this man, she won't want to leave London, will she?'

Francis smiled. 'The owner of the agency where she works owes me a few favours. So, if she wants to be kept on the books there, she'll accept the position at your farm. Besides, it's only for a few weeks.'

'And, in the meantime, you try to buy off this Mr Unsuitable?' Callum guessed.

'I suppose you could put it like that.' Francis shuffled the contract that lay between them on the table. 'What do you say? Have we got a deal?'

The distant sound of a car coming down the driveway sent Callum to the living-room window. The afternoon sun was starting to go down, lighting the hills and the sweep of the green valley in a rosy haze. A few birds perched in the bare, winter branches of the old oak tree flapped noisily away as the roar of the engine grew louder. Then, as Callum watched, a shiny red sports car thundered over the cattle grid and pulled up outside.

'Is that her, Daddy?' Alice asked in a small breathless voice from behind him.

'I believe it is.' Callum watched as one well-shod foot appeared from the vehicle. The first things he noticed were the high heels, then the long shapely legs. The grey trouser suit was unmistakably designer chic, and would have looked stunning in the streets of Kensington, but was definitely out of place here. Then he noticed the complex style of her honey-blonde hair, woven into a perfect French plait. She looked as if she had spent all morning at the hairdressers. Just what he needed, Callum thought in disgust, a prima donna, and at one of the farm's busiest periods.

He should never have agreed to Francis Bernard's crazy scheme. To hell with the extra money, he had a business to run. This wasn't a damn crèche for demented Sloane Rangers.

Callum watched with mounting incredulity as she proceeded to take several matching designer suitcases from the back of the car.

Hells bells, he thought, with rising panic as the suitcases kept appearing like some kind of conjuring trick from the small trunk of the car. Francis had to be having him on. This woman couldn't possibly have come here with any intention of working. She obviously thought she was on some kind of 'slumming it' vacation: the type the upper class went on for a bit of a hoot, in between swinging off chandeliers and champagne binges.

He'd have to tell her to go. He'd ring Francis and apologise. Then he remembered how sick and how worried the man was, and felt torn.

'Daddy?' Alice was pulling on his sleeve. 'Pick me up. I want to see.'

Callum looked down at the five-year-old and noticed absently that her pink pinafore dress was on back to front. Ellen must have been rushing when she changed her out of her school uniform.

'Is she pretty? Does she look like Mary Poppins?' Alice asked, her blue eyes wide.

'Not quite, darling,' Callum answered with a smile, hoisting the child up into his arms.

'Don't see why she should get so excited,' Kyle muttered without looking up from his sprawled position in front of the TV. 'We have Granny Ellen and Millie to look after us. We don't need anyone else.'

Callum looked over at his son. 'Grandma needs a bit of a rest,' he found himself saying, and then frowned as he wondered how far from the truth that actually was. He wondered if it was his imagination, or had Ellen looked a little relieved when he had told her he was getting someone else in for a few weeks.

The doorbell rang making all of them jump. 'Come on, now, Kyle, switch the TV off. I want you on your best behaviour for our guest.'

Kyle ignored him and, instead, swung his legs, in the grey school shorts, backwards and forwards narrowly missing the glass of lemonade on the coffee table.

The doorbell rang again.

Outside, Zoë tapped her foot with annoyance. It was freezing out here, what were they doing inside? The cold, however, was completely forgotten as the door swung open and she found herself looking up at an extremely handsome man.

He was dressed in jeans and a beige crew neck jumper, and was probably about thirty-three or -four. Tall, broad, with thick dark hair and dark eyes, he possessed the type of rugged masculinity that made Zoë feel as if she'd stepped onto a film set. George Clooney eat your heart out, she thought dazedly.

'Callum Langston?' she asked, trying to sound nonchalant.

'Yes.' His eyes raked over her, disturbing her cool façade even further.

'Hi, I'm Zoë Bernard.'

'I kind of guessed that,' he murmured, his eyes moving from her red lips to the well-manicured bright red nails. She was undoubtedly attractive...in fact, maybe a little too attractive for a man's peace of mind. But, as for cleaning, looking after his children and running the farm kitchen, he may as well ring Ellen and beg her to come back right now.

Her green eyes narrowed. 'So? Are you going to invite me in, or don't I pass the doorstep test?' she asked, wondering if she had imagined that sarcasm in his deep sexy voice. 'I have just driven all the way up from London and I could do with a cup of tea.'

'Sorry.' He stood back and allowed her to walk in. A huge roaring fire warmed the room. Two young children were sitting on the settee, a cute little girl of about five with blonde pigtails and wide excited eyes. And a sullen-looking boy of about eight with dark unruly hair, wearing a grey school uniform.

'Hello.' Zoë smiled at them both. The little girl smiled back, but the boy just continued to stare at her. 'I'm missing my favourite programme on TV because of you,' he accused suddenly.

'Oh, dear!' Zoë glanced at the TV and noticed it had been unplugged from the wall.

'Kyle, give me a hand with Miss Bernard's cases, please,' his father asked in a quiet tone.

For a second, Zoë thought the child was going to ignore his father, but then he got up and trotted outside with him obediently.

'You've come to look after us, haven't you?' the little girl said crossing her legs and looking up at her in a manner that was disconcertingly adult and at complete odds with the back-to-front pinafore dress. 'Granny Ellen needed a rest, you know. We were making her tired.'

'Were you? I'm sure you didn't mean to.'

'No. But Kyle's a bit of a handful.'

'Really?' Zoë tried not to smile.

The child wrinkled her nose in deep concentration. 'Do you live in London?'

'Yes, I do.'

'Do you know the Queen?'

'Not personally, no.'

'Alice, leave Miss Bernard alone. She's too tired for an inquisition, just now,' Callum said, bringing in the suit-cases.

'I don't mind.' Zoë smiled at the little girl. 'And you can call me Zoë.'

'I'll show you up to your room.' Callum watched as Kyle struggled in with a large vanity case. She had to have enough make-up in there to paint the house, he thought dryly, reaching to take it from the boy. 'Right, this way.' He nodded towards the stairs.

Zoë followed him up the narrow twisting stairway and then down a long dark corridor. Alice and Kyle trailed be-hind.

Zoë loved the farmhouse. It was very old, and full of character. The floorboards creaked as they walked and seemed to be very uneven as if they were walking up and down instead of in a straight line. The doors were low and she noticed that Callum had to bend his head as he led the way into her bedroom.

It was a large room dominated by a huge wooden bed and dark wardrobes. Like the lounge, it had the faded air of beauty in need of a few loving touches to restore it to its former glory. A fresh coat of paint, some up-to-date soft furnishings and it would be absolutely delightful, she thought.

'Wow, it's hot in here,' Zoë remarked, putting a hand on the radiator.

'Well, it's only early spring and I do like to keep the house warm.' Callum put her luggage down. 'But I'll adjust it for you.' He crossed to the control at the side of the radiator as Zoë went across to one of the two windows built into the deep walls.

The view out over the fells was spectacular. Good

enough to paint. She might have a go while she was here. She'd brought all her art equipment.

She fiddled with the catch on the window and opened it noticing, as she did, that they were the original, stylish sash windows. 'There, that's better.' She turned and smiled at Callum. 'You could have grown orchids in here.'

He didn't wholeheartedly return her smile. He seemed to be looking at her with a hint of circumspection in the darkness of his eyes.

'You live in a beautiful part of the world,' she murmured, trying to lighten the atmosphere. 'I've always loved the Lake District. My mother used to bring me up here for weekends when I was little.'

For a moment she looked sad, Callum thought as he watched her. Her skin was very pale; her wide green eyes, fringed with thick dark lashes, seemed shadowed, vulnerable.

Then she smiled at him again and the green eyes were filled with a purpose and confidence that made the notion foolish. Zoë was a woman who could have the world silverplated if she wanted it. She had never had a real problem in her life. Daddy was there, picking up the pieces.

He moved her suitcase nearer to the wardrobe. 'Is there anything you need?' he asked politely.

'I don't think so.' She crossed and sat down on the bed. It was very hard: no give in it at all. A bit like Callum Langston, she thought as she watched him. She wasn't used to men who didn't return her smile. Usually there was some flicker of admiration in a man's eyes when he looked at her, but Callum seemed to regard her as if she was some kind of creature who had descended on him from outer space. He had a wonderful physique though, she thought, allowing her eyes to linger at the breadth of his shoulders before moving down the lithe frame. Yes, very nice. Her flatmate, Honey, would adore Callum. She was a dancer with incredibly long legs, always bemoaning the fact that it was hard to find a tall handsome man. Yes, Honey would certainly approve of Callum.

She transferred her attention to the two children who stood just inside the doorway watching her. Alice seemed a sweetheart; Kyle was a bit like his father, wary, maybe even hostile.

'Granny Ellen will be coming back soon,' he said as her eyes lighted on him.

'Yes, I'm just filling in for her, am I?' she said cheerfully. 'You'll have to help me and tell me what I'm supposed to do.'

Kyle just stared at her with reproachful eyes.

What was going through his mind? Zoë wondered.

'I'll run through our schedule with you once you've freshened up,' Callum answered for them. He moved towards the door as the phone rang downstairs. 'I'll leave you to unpack. Come on, kids, let's give Zoë some space.' He took Kyle's hand as he went out of the room, but Alice remained, her eyes wide and watchful.

'Alice.' Her father called from the staircase but she didn't hurry after him.

'Do you like Barbie?' she asked Zoë as if it was a tremendously important question and Zoë's future depended urgently on the reply.

'I love her,' Zoë answered solemnly.

Alice smiled. 'So do I.'

Zoë stood up from the bed and opened up some of her cases to unpack.

She took out several dresses and opened up the voluminous wardrobes. There was women's clothing hanging in there already.

'They belong to Mummy,' Alice said softly. 'The wardrobe next to it is empty though.'

Zoë's eyes flicked over the rails of clothing before she

closed the door quickly. Her boss had told her that Callum was a widower. She wondered how long ago it was since his wife had died. It seemed sad still having her clothes hanging in the wardrobes.

As Alice had pointed out, the wardrobe next to it was empty. She started to hang a few things up.

'What's this, Zoë?'

Alice's inquisitive little voice made her turn around to find the little girl on her hands and knees down by her vanity case going through her watercolours.

'That's my paint box. I like to paint pictures in my spare time.'

'I like painting too,' Alice said. Before Zoë could stop her, she had unscrewed the top off one of the tubes and vermilion red squished out over tiny fingers.

'Oh, dear!' Alice looked over at Zoë, a horrified expression on her face.

'It doesn't matter.' Zoë was quick to reassure her. 'It will wash off.' She made a mental note to keep the box locked in future as she took her sponge bag out of the case. 'Come and show me where the bathroom is and I'll help you clean up.'

The bathroom was huge and very luxurious. It had the original white Victorian freestanding bath and big brass taps, heated towel rails and thick peach towels to match the carpet.

'Where do you sleep, Alice?' Zoë asked as they walked back out to the corridor.

'My bedroom is across here,' Alice pushed another door open.

The child's room was warmly inviting, a cosy patchwork bedspread on the bed, books and toys lining the shelves. 'And Kyle's is here.' Happily, Alice fell into the role of tour guide and grabbed hold of Zoë's hand, showing her into a room that was similarly welcoming. Zoë noticed the photographs beside the bed and walked over to have a closer look. They were all of the children when they were younger and an attractive woman with long dark hair.

'That's my mummy,' Alice said proudly.

'Yes, I thought it must be. She's very pretty.'

'She's up in heaven now,' Alice said matter-of-factly.

Zoë felt a pang of sadness as she studied the woman with the laughing blue eyes and the windswept hair, her arms tightly around her children.

'And this is where Daddy sleeps.' Before Zoë realised it, the child was leading her into the room directly opposite her own.

A pile of books sat on the table next to an enormous four-poster bed. A desk with a lamp sat in the window, strewn with what looked like accounts.

'What on earth are you doing in here?' Callum's voice coming from behind them made Zoë wheel around.

'Sorry.' She smiled at him. 'Alice thought she should familiarise me with the layout of the house.'

'Well, let's not get too familiar.' Callum held his door for her pointedly.

Zoë's eyebrows lifted. 'Sorry,' she murmured, walking past him with haste.

Honestly, the man took himself far too seriously. As if she was interested in his damn bedroom. She wouldn't have gone in except for Alice.

As soon as she had left the room, Callum hurried over to his desk and picked up one of the letters lying there. When he had seen Zoë in here, he had remembered with horror this letter from her father lying open on his desk. In it, Francis Bernard was joyfully telling him that Zoë's boss had made sure she would be accepting the temporary job as housekeeper and carer for his children. He had set down the date she would be arriving, plus a request for Callum to try to keep his daughter at the farmhouse for longer than two weeks. 'Use some ingenuity,' Francis had urged.

What did the man expect him to do? Callum wondered in agitation. Tie the woman up? It was absurd. He wished he'd never agreed to the ridiculous charade in the first place.

He opened a drawer and stuck the letter inside out of sight. Two weeks was all he was prepared to give Francis Bernard's scheme. Apart from anything else, he had the disturbing notion that Zoë Bernard was trouble with a capital T.

# CHAPTER TWO

WHEN Zoë went downstairs a little while later, it was nearing six o'clock. She followed the sound of voices along the corridor and found herself in a large rustic-style kitchen.

Callum was on the phone. Alice was sitting at the kitchen table colouring in.

'I've got to go out,' Callum said, without any preamble, as he put the phone down. 'Can you see to the children's dinner? And check they've done their homework?'

'Yes,' Zoë answered him quietly. She couldn't help feeling that instead of rushing off like this he should have been taking time to talk to her about her job. 'But I was hoping we could discuss the extent of my duties, the children's schedule and—'

'We'll do that later.' He grabbed his keys from the pine sideboard and then reached for a coat that hung beside the back door. 'Bedtime is eight for Alice. Eight-thirty for Kyle.'

A black collie dog jumped up from underneath the table to follow his master to the door. Callum paused suddenly. 'You will be able to manage, won't you?'

'Yes, of course,' Zoë replied indignantly. 'I'm an excellent cook and I have a diploma in child care. That's why you are paying me, isn't it?'

Why was he looking at her with such indecision? Zoë wondered. 'My boss, Martin Fellows, forwarded my references to you, didn't he?'

'Yes.' For a second, Callum still hesitated. Then he sighed. She certainly had an air of capability about her. 'Any trouble at all, ring Ellen.' He went across to the phone to scribble down her number. 'She's only a short drive away.'

He kissed the top of Alice's head as he walked past. 'Be good for Zoë,' he murmured. Then he was gone.

Zoë strolled to the back door and watched through the glass as he allowed the dog to jump into the back of his Land Rover before climbing in himself.

Where was he going in such a hurry? she wondered. Behind him, the sky was tinged with pink as the sun slowly disappeared behind the mountains to be replaced with the cold hard glitter of frost on the ground.

'Where is your daddy going?' Zoë asked Alice.

'Work. The little lambs are being born, so sometimes he has to go out late,' she replied without looking up from her work.

It was lambing time, of course. She had noticed there were a few in the fields as she drove along the country lanes today.

Zoë turned and looked around the kitchen. It was somewhat untidy with piles of dishes in the sink and the counter tops cluttered with papers and cups. But apart from that, it was a lovely, family, farmhouse kitchen. The cupboards were pine, the floor tiled in a dark quarry stone and a huge green Rayburn sent out a lot of warmth.

She'd soon have this place restored to order, she thought. But first, she would see to the children's dinner. 'What would you like to eat tonight?' she asked, walking across to look in the fridge.

'Sausage and chips?' Alice asked hopefully.

'What did you have for lunch?' Zoë asked, her head in the fridge.

'Pizza and chips.'

'Hmm. Then, how about a shepherd's pie for supper?' Zoë turned towards the fridge. 'That's if I can find some meat.'

'Oh, yes.' Alice jumped down from her chair and ran to open the deep-freeze. 'Look, there are lots of things in here,' she said helpfully.

'Thank you.' Zoë smiled at the little girl, and started to take some things out. 'Where is your brother?' she asked as she went over to look at the microwave.

'Outside.'

'Outside?' Zoë paused. 'Why would he be outside?'

'Don't know.' Alice shrugged.

Zoë hurried over to the back door. The farmyard was in pitch darkness now. Dark, cold, and probably filled with dangerous places where an eight-year-old could meet with a very serious accident.

'Didn't your father see him going outside?'

'I don't think so.'

Wrenching open the back door, Zoë called loudly, 'Kyle please come in, I'm worried about you.'

There was no reply, just a low moo from one of the outbuildings. The frost was so sharp that it caught at Zoë's throat. 'Kyle, please,' she called again.

The moon sailed out from behind a cloud and she could make out the shadowy outlines of the barn and the out-houses. No sign of Kyle.

'Are you sure he isn't in the house?' She closed the door and crossed towards the hall to look.

Where was he? Zoë wondered after a thorough search of each room revealed no child. Her heart thundering against her chest, she headed downstairs. She imagined Callum's fury when he returned to find she had lost his son. God, she'd only been here for one afternoon. She remembered his hesitation to leave, the way he had looked at her, as if deep down he didn't think she was at all capable. But she was very capable, and responsible. This wasn't her fault.

She opened the back door again. 'Kyle, if you don't get

in here this minute there is going to be big trouble,' she called.

The only answer was the eerie cry of some kind of bird.

Callum glanced at his watch and then down at the dead ewe beside him. They'd fought for nearly an hour to save her, but to no avail. Then they'd tried to get her two orphaned lambs accepted by another of the ewes. This had also ended in failure. All in all, a bad day, Callum thought dourly as he watched the lambs nudge at the dead mother, their pitiful beats filling the freezing night air. Callum picked them up and placed them under the warmth of his jacket.

'I think we'll call it a night, Tom. We can't do anything more here.'

'More's the pity.' Tom shook his head sadly.

'I'll come back up at first light.' Callum turned to lead the way back down the mountainside. In the distance, he could see the lights of the farmhouse blazing, like a welcoming beacon. He was tired and hungry. He was also worried about the children. He hadn't liked leaving them with Zoë Bernard. Yes, her references were excellent, her father was a decent man, and she seemed OK. But he didn't really know her, did he? He'd only been out for two and a half hours. He wanted to stay longer; he knew there were other sheep he needed to check on. But usually he had Ellen staying at the farm, and he knew the children were fine with her.

'Do you want me to stay on?' Tom asked.

Callum glanced gratefully at the young labourer. 'Thanks, but you've worked long enough hours today. You get off, I'll see you in the morning.'

Callum patted him on the back before they went their separate ways.

The farm was silent as Callum stepped in the back door.

He noticed that the kitchen was immaculately tidy, the dirty dishes were gone, the worktops gleamed. He was quite taken aback, he really hadn't expected Zoë to do so much.

He put the lambs down in the basket next to the Rayburn and then went to wash his hands before going upstairs to check on the children.

Alice was tucked up in her bed, fast asleep. The red glow of the night-lamp highlighted the cosy patchwork quilt and the teddy bears on the bed.

Callum walked next door to look in on his son. The bedside lamp was still on. Kyle was lying on his side with his back to the door.

'Kyle?'

There was no answer. Yet Callum had the distinct impression the child was not asleep. 'Kyle, is everything OK?' he asked gently. There was still no reply. Callum pulled the covers closer around the child and then turned out the light. 'See you in the morning,' he murmured reaching to give him a kiss.

He almost walked into Zoë as he emerged from the bedroom. She was carrying the laundry basket from the bathroom. 'You made me jump. I didn't hear you come in,' she said almost dropping it.

He took the basket from her noting, as he did, that Kyle's school uniform was in there and it looked as if it was covered in soot.

'Were the kids OK for you?' he asked casually.

She hesitated. 'Yes, they were fine.'

'You've got soot or something on your face,' he observed.

'Have I?' She put a hand to the wrong cheek. He noticed that it shook slightly.

'Here.' He leaned across and rubbed at the grey smudge on the smooth pallor of her cheek.

For some reason the touch of his skin against hers disturbed her. For a moment, her eyes held with his. He was standing very close, so close that she could see the golden dark shadows in his eyes, the faint traces of lines at the side of them. Laughter lines, lines to show he had lived and loved.

Her gaze moved to the sensual curve of his lips, enticingly male, provocatively close. Her stomach felt as if it was contracting sharply with some tug of emotion she couldn't understand.

'There.' He stepped back. 'What have you been doing? Digging for coal?'

She remembered the horror of not being able to find Kyle and the memory kicked everything else out of her. The child had terrified her. She'd searched for over an hour. Eventually she had found him, of all places, in the cellar with the coal. He had been deliberately hiding from her, had heard her calling to him, and had ignored her.

To make matters worse he had been lying on the floor and had been covered in black soot. When she had demanded a reason for his naughty behaviour he had just stared at her, sullen defiance in his eyes.

Was it just a childish prank, or was there something deeper behind the behaviour? she wondered now. And should she tell Callum?

'Zoë?' Callum's voice made her return her attention to him.

Maybe not, she thought, noting the serious light in his eyes. Maybe telling tales wasn't the way to handle the situation. She'd have a quiet word with the child tomorrow when they had both calmed down.

'I was just…clearing up a bit.' She walked past him towards the stairs. 'I made sausage and chips for the children. Do you want me to make some for you?'

'No, thanks. I'll make myself a sandwich later.' He followed her downstairs and into the kitchen and put the laundry basket down. 'I'm sorry I had to drop you in the deep end and rush off like that.'

'It's OK. Alice told me that it's a busy time for you.' She sorted the washing out and crouched down to bundle it into the machine. Then she looked down in surprise as a lamb nudged at her elbow. 'A product of your evening?' she asked.

'Yes, but not a very successful evening as the mother died.' He took out a large container of milk from the fridge and poured it into a pan. 'Which means we will have to bottle feed, and keep them warm in here for a while.'

He watched as she petted the animal.

'Have you had something to eat?' he asked.

'Yes, I ate with the children.'

She got up and watched as he poured the milk into two bottles through a funnel.

'Do you want me to do that while you get yourself a sandwich?'

'Thanks.' He screwed on the caps.

'Then maybe you can tell me why you've recruited a home help through an agency in London? Wasn't there one in Kendal, or Carlisle?'

Callum nearly dropped the bottle on the floor as he passed it to her. Did she guess there was something fishy going on? 'A friend recommended your agency to me.'

She was sidetracked away from the conversation as she sat down at the kitchen table and took one of the lambs on her knee. It wriggled and wouldn't take the teat in its mouth.

Callum grinned as he watched her struggle. 'Here.' He came across and caught hold of the lamb, opening its mouth for her. As soon as it tasted the milk, it sucked greedily, pulling sharply on the bottle.

Then he picked up the other lamb and leaned against the counter top as he fed it the bottle with an ease born of long experience. 'I can see you are well used to this,' Zoë remarked.

'Every year we have a few to look after. Thanks for tidying up in here by the way.' He changed the subject abruptly. 'I didn't expect you to do so much on your first night.'

'It was no problem,' she said lightly and had to smile to herself. The truth was that because of Kyle's prank she had been running around like a woman possessed to get this place straight before he got back, which was why she hadn't got around to making the shepherd's pie she had planned.

The wind was getting up outside. It whistled around the house, filling the silence between them.

Zoë glanced up at him. She wondered how long it was since his wife had died. 'I gather that I'm standing in for the children's grandmother? Is she ill or something?'

'She just needed a rest.'

'And you have a housekeeper, Alice was telling me.'

'Yes. Millie comes in twice a week, so you can have two days off, if that suits?'

Zoë nodded. 'I won't be here very long, so I'll just fit in around you.'

A strand of hair had escaped from her severe hairstyle and it curled around her face. She looked very young, he thought suddenly. He wondered if the guy she was seeing in London was as bad as her father had painted him. 'If I need you to stay longer, would that be possible?'

She hesitated. 'Well, maybe a few days, but not much more. To be honest, I've taken this job as a favour to Martin…he owns the agency,' she explained. 'But I really need to be back in London by the second week of April.'

'A heavy date, or another job?' He tried to sound casually indifferent. It was, after all, none of his business.

'A bit of both.' She smiled at him. She had a lovely

smile, warm and genuine; it lit her eyes and made them sparkle with life and enthusiasm. He found himself thinking how delightful she was, then pulled himself up. How could he find himself drawn to a woman who was supposed to be nothing more than a social butterfly? He frowned. Except she didn't seem a bit like Francis had described.

The lamb finished its bottle and she put it down beside the Rayburn. 'Perhaps you could go through a list of what you want me to do while I'm here,' she said in an authoritative tone.

This woman was starting to bear no resemblance at all to the woman he had been expecting. With difficulty, he put his analysis of her character to one side. 'Mainly, I want you to look after the children. Take them to school and tidy up, organise dinner for them. As you can see, I'm a bit tied up with the farm at the moment, so I'd appreciate you watching them some evenings as well. If you want to go out any night, tell me the day before and I'll organise a babysitter.'

'I don't think I'll be going out in the evenings. I don't know anyone up here.'

He nodded. 'Just as long as you know that you're not a prisoner in the house.' As he said the words, a pang of guilt struck him. If her father had his way, she would be a prisoner here for longer than just a few weeks. Still, her father had her best interests at heart, Callum reminded himself.

'I'll do the school run with you in the morning,' he said. 'Familiarise you with everything. We'll have to leave here about eight-fifteen.' He put the lamb back down on the floor. 'Would you like a cup of tea?'

'No, thanks, I'm going to turn in. I'm really tired.' As she stood up, she noticed he was getting out hot-water bottles. 'The nights get cold here, I take it?' she asked with a grin.

'They do. But this is for them.' Callum nodded towards

the lambs. 'There is an electric blanket in the cupboard if you want it?'

'I don't think I'll need it, but thanks anyway.' She hesitated. 'Do you mind if I use your phone? I'll go through the operator and pay you for the call. It's just that my mobile won't work up here.'

Callum hesitated. Was she going to ring the unsuitable boyfriend? Her father wouldn't be too keen on that. On the other hand, he couldn't say no, it would seem very callous and mean.

Her green eyes held his steadily. 'Is it OK?' she asked again.

'Yes, but don't be on long, I'm expecting a call.'

As he turned to make himself something to eat, he could hear her dialling on the phone in the hall.

'Hi, it's me.' Her voice was soft and honeyed. 'I was thinking about you. How's it going?'

Callum banged a cupboard door and coughed so that she would be aware that he could hear.

She didn't seem to care. 'Don't be silly. I'll be back in two weeks…you can wait that long.'

Callum frowned. He really didn't want to hear this.

She laughed. She had a very sexy laugh, Callum noted. Yes, she had to be speaking to her boyfriend. 'I'll look forward to it,' she murmured.

What would she look forward to? Callum wondered. He wrenched open the cutlery drawer.

'Listen, I can't talk now, I'll ring you tomorrow. Oh…by the way…have you heard anything from my father?'

Callum's movements stilled.

'No? I just wondered. OK, see you, honey.'

Honey? Callum pulled a face.

She put her head back around the door. 'Thanks, Callum. See you in the morning.'

'Yes, goodnight.'

When Zoë went into her bedroom she found the curtains were billowing in the breeze from the open window. Hurriedly she went across to close it.

Then she sat at the dressing table and brushed her hair. It was cold in the room now, and she almost wished she had taken Callum's offer of the electric blanket. She turned up the radiator before changing into her nightdress, then dived under the quilt and lay there shivering.

When she switched out the light, the room was pitch dark. The only sound was the wind whistling around the house. She was used to streetlights and the noise of cars. It was strange hearing nothing but the elements. She lay and stared up into the blackness.

A blood-curdling cry from outside made her sit bolt upright. What on earth was that? There was silence followed by the rattle of the wind on the windows. She lay back down, her heart banging against her chest. It had definitely come from outside. Was it some kind of animal?

She heard the sound of footsteps on the stairs and the creak of the floorboards.

The cry pierced the night air again. It sounded like a soul in torment. At the same time there was an almighty bang from the window, and the curtains flapped into the room on a stream of cold air. Zoë flung back the covers of her bed and raced across to investigate.

'Zoë? Are you OK? What was that noise?' Callum asked from outside her bedroom door.

'The window seems to have shot open.' She struggled to pull the casement up, but it wouldn't budge. She left it and went to open her bedroom door.

The light from the corridor was reassuringly welcome as was the sight of Callum.

'I don't know what happened,' she said. 'One moment I was lying in bed, the next there was a strange noise and the window flew open.'

His eyes moved over her, taking in the tumble of long blonde hair around her shoulders and the wide green eyes, before moving to the delicate soft curves of her body in the revealing, black silk nightdress. She certainly was extremely attractive, he thought distractedly.

'There it is again,' she said as another cry came faintly through the air. 'What the hell is it?'

He smiled. 'It's Percy,' he said calmly.

'Who the hell is Percy?' She shivered with cold.

'He's a peacock.'

'A peacock?'

'Big bird, nice tail.' He enlightened her mockingly. 'Don't worry, he's not dangerous and he hardly ever breaks into women's bedrooms.'

'Ha ha,' Zoë grated unevenly. She felt foolish now and that in turn made her angry. 'You could have warned me you had a menagerie outside.'

'Hardly that, but you are on a farm,' he reminded her wryly.

Zoë's eyes narrowed. 'I know I'm a city girl, Callum, but I do know that a peacock isn't a farm animal.'

'Do you?' He smiled, then walked past her into her bedroom. 'Let's see if I can fix this window for you.'

She watched from the doorway and couldn't help feeling pleased when he struggled as much as she had to close the offending casement.

'Strong man like you, I'd have thought you could have closed that, no problem,' she murmured sardonically, enjoying the opportunity to get her own back on his patronising attitude of a few moments ago.

'The catch has gone,' he muttered. 'Must have been the wind.' He gave up his attempts and turned his attention back to her. Then he grinned. 'OK, I'm not the strong man I thought I was. I need tools to fix this particular problem.'

'Excuses, excuses,' she bantered lightly and shook her head.

He laughed and held up his hands. 'OK, I shouldn't have made fun of you.'

'No, you shouldn't…' She grinned. 'Big mistake.'

'Well, all I can say is, I'm sorry.'

Suddenly she was acutely conscious of the way he was looking at her and her state of undress. She should have put on a dressing gown before dashing out the door, she thought belatedly.

He moved towards her. 'So, have we got a truce?'

He was incredibly sexy, she thought. She may have been making fun about his body, but it was extremely delectable. Very masculine and powerful, and that gleam in his eye as he'd looked at her, half teasing, half serious, had made her pulses start to race.

'Yes, a truce,' she murmured backing away a little from him.

'Good, and maybe you should sleep in my room tonight,' he suggested casually.

Her eyebrows rose.

'I mean it might be best if we swap rooms, temporarily,' he drawled with a grin.

She felt a dull flush creep up under her cheekbones. 'I know what you mean,' she assured him hastily, trying to drag her mind away from the outrageously seductive thoughts that had just flicked through it.

'Come on, then. Let's get this organised.' He led the way across the landing and into his room. It was warm and inviting after the chill of her room. 'The sheets are fresh,' he said waving a hand towards his bed. 'Millie did all the bedrooms this morning.'

She stood just inside the door and watched as he opened drawers and took out some clothes.

'What about you?' she asked suddenly, feeling guilty.

He was probably exhausted. He'd worked until late and he hadn't eaten properly. 'You can't sleep in that windswept room.'

'Are you inviting me to stay in here with you?' He slanted her that teasing look again that made her senses spin.

She tried very hard not to blush. 'Don't be silly.'

'Then, I'll have to sleep over there, won't I?' He grinned. 'Don't worry, I'm used to roughing it. I'll try to wedge the window up with something and I'll sort it out in the morning.'

It was only when the door closed behind him that Zoë remembered that she didn't have her dressing gown or any of her personal belongings from her room.

About to go after him, she changed her mind. It could wait until the morning.

She slipped into the bed. It was blissfully comfortable, much better than the one she'd just come from. She looked around the room. The walls were a pale buttermilk colour, the carpet the same. The only splashes of colour were the pictures, all of gardens filled with blossom. A woman had chosen them, Zoë thought. She turned and her gaze fell on the framed photograph of the children next to the bed. It couldn't be easy for Callum bringing them up on his own, she thought as she reached to switch off the light.

She closed her eyes and thought about her own father. He had brought her up on his own. She'd been about Kyle's age when her mother had died, but she still remembered very clearly how bewildered she had felt.

Her father had done his best. She sighed as she thought about Francis. If only he could let go now, allow her to live her life without always interfering. He just couldn't accept that she wanted to be independent. Wanted to work and carve out a niche for herself without his help. He was forever meddling in her affairs. It drove her crazy. They'd had a terrible argument about it a couple of weeks ago. And they still hadn't made it up properly. That's why she had rung her flatmate tonight, hoping he would have rung to speak to her. But Honey had said there were no messages. Except one from Matthew Devine telling her not to worry and everything was on schedule.

She rolled over and buried her head in the pillows as a feeling of excitement washed through her. Matthew was an art dealer and he was helping with her first ever art exhibition. She was hoping this was going to be a turning point for her and that, afterwards, she would be able to give up working for the temping agency and work full-time on her pictures.

Matthew had been a marvellous encouragement. She knew he had a somewhat shady past, but all that was a long time ago, way before she had met him and he was a reformed character now. They occasionally went out on dates but, although he was extremely charismatic, theirs wasn't a serious relationship, more a deep friendship. She hadn't told her father that, though. She had deliberately let him think that her relationship with Matt was more serious, because she knew if her father got wind of the exhibition she was planning he would send his friends and his work colleagues to buy her pictures and she would never know if success was something she could have achieved on her own.

She turned over and stared up at the ceiling. Maybe, instead of letting her father think she was serious about Matt, she should have told him the truth. But, then, Francis had never been too pleased about her love of art anyway. He would have preferred her to take an interest in the family business. If the truth was known, she was just a big disappointment to him and she was sorry about that.

But it was her life, and these were her decisions.

She loved him dearly but she refused to tolerate his domineering ways any longer. She punched the pillow in frustration. His reaction when he had thought she was serious about Matthew had been very predictable. He had totally blown a gasket.

Well, she was old enough to make up her own mind. He should realise that, and she wasn't going to speak to him until he apologised. When she did decide to get married, she would chose her own partner. She had been shocked speechless when he had told her he had someone in mind for her! He'd always been a bit autocratic but he had gone too far this time.

She turned over again. Let him fret now, she told herself fiercely. Let him think she was going to marry Matthew Devine. Serve him right.

She wasn't going to back down and she wasn't going to ring him. She had to make a stand, show him that she was living her own life on her own terms.

# CHAPTER THREE

IT WAS pitch-black when something hurled itself onto the bed. Zoë sat up, disorientated. She couldn't remember where she was.

'Time to get up, Daddy,' a young voice sang. 'It's six-thirty.'

'It's the middle of the night,' Zoë groaned, switching on the light.

Two young faces stared back at her. Alice looked surprised, Kyle looked horrified.

'What are you doing in my daddy's bed?' he demanded angrily.

'We've swapped rooms,' Zoë answered. She glanced, bleary eyed, at her watch. 'Do you always get up so early?'

'Always,' Alice answered happily.

The children went rushing off to see their father and Zoë gingerly put a foot out from under the covers. She hadn't woken up properly; it felt like the most ungodly hour. She padded out into the corridor and along to the bathroom. A shower was what she needed.

She struggled to turn on the shower over the bath, but finally managed to get a full jet of hot water. Then she slipped out of the silk nightdress, adjusted the shower curtain so that the floor wouldn't get wet and stepped in.

Bliss, she thought as she pushed back the heavy weight of blonde hair and lifted her face up to the full force of the water. Warmth flowed in pounding rivulets over her body. She lifted her arms and stretched. 'Wonderful,' she purred.

Callum pulled on jeans and a thick jumper. He'd have a look at the catch on the window before work, he thought.

But first, he went to check on the children. Since they had left his bedroom they had been very quiet.

Mid way down the corridor he heard the shower and noticed the bathroom door was ajar. He walked in, then stopped dead as he saw Zoë stark naked in the shower. She had her arms up in the air. The honey-bronze skin was wet and soapy. Her blonde hair swung down to the small, nipped-in waist. Her bottom was shapely and pert and her legs seemed to stretch for ever.

He turned to go, embarrassed at his intrusion then, mesmerised, he watched as she hummed to herself and reached blindly for the soap.

He smiled and, for a moment, was tempted to go over and hand her the bar of soap just for the sheer hell of it.

'It's wonderful and marvellous,' she sang in a breathy high voice, finally finding the soap and starting to rub it over her body in a way that made Callum's blood pressure, amongst other things, rise.

'I agree that the view isn't bad,' he drawled turning to leave. 'But I think you should lock the door in future.'

Zoë whirled around in shock and, through a watery haze, was just in time to see him closing the door behind him.

She stood still, her heart pounding in mortification. She hadn't locked the door! What had she been thinking of? But surely he had heard the shower; he could have knocked on the door, called out to see if she was in there.

Angrily she turned off the water and reached for a towel. There wasn't one. She peered around and observed with dismay that the towels were wet on the floor and the only dry one was a tiny hand one next to the sink.

'Damn it all,' she muttered, stepping out of the bath and reaching for it. She tried to dry herself, but her hair had got soaked when she'd turned around and now it dripped all over her. As fast as she dried she was getting wet again. In frustration, she reached for her nightdress and put it on.

It clung to her damp body, sticking uncomfortably to her breasts.

Surreptitiously she opened the bathroom door and peered down the corridor. No one was about. She ran down towards her room, closing the door behind her with relief. The feeling was short-lived, however, as she saw Callum in there, trying to fix the window.

He glanced at her, his eyes flicking over the revealing curves of her body in the wet nightdress.

'I think you should take your clothes and move temporarily into my room,' he said, nonchalantly turning his attention back to the window as if they spent every morning together with her in a state of undress.

The window was open and it was freezing in the room. She shivered violently and wasn't about to argue. 'OK.' She looked around for her dressing gown. 'And next time you come into the bathroom, please knock,' she told him frostily.

'I'm sorry. I thought one of the children had left the shower on. It's something they do.' He sat on the window sill and looked at her. There was a gleam of amusement in his dark eyes. 'There are towels in the airing cupboard in the corridor.'

He couldn't help but notice that she was well-endowed; her body was round and ripe in all the right places.

Frowning at the thought, he turned his attention back to what he was doing. She was the daughter of his friend; he couldn't allow himself to think like that. He was supposed to be keeping her safe from an unsuitable man, not coveting her for himself. Anyway, she wasn't his type, he told himself fiercely.

Aware that she was moving around the room, gathering up her belongings, he tried to stop himself from looking at her again. She was a rich girl, all cashmere and silk, shallow and spoilt, according to her father. He frowned as, once again, that portrayal jarred on him.

Out of the corner of his eye he could see her putting on her dressing gown. Then she seemed to be searching around for something.

Still he didn't look around.

'You haven't seen the belt to my dressing gown lying about anywhere, have you?' she asked after a while.

'Sorry, I haven't.'

She was standing by his tool box. He could see her toes poking out beneath the long dressing gown. They were painted a bright scarlet red. She probably spent all her days in beauty parlours, he told himself briskly. 'Will you pass me a bradawl from that box while you're there?' he asked absently.

She bent down, scrabbled amongst the contents of the box, and handed it to him.

'Thanks.' He closed the window with a sharp thud.

'Are you sure you haven't seen the belt of my dressing gown?'

'Quite sure. Will you pass me a screwdriver?'

'What do you want, a crosshead or an ordinary one?' she asked bending to get it for him.

'Do you know the difference?' he asked with a frown.

'Are you trying to be funny?'

'No…' He grinned as he met the annoyed gleam in her green eyes. 'After last night, I've learnt my lesson. I'll have the crosshead.'

She grinned and put it into his hand before turning away to continue with her search.

Callum stared at the screwdriver in his hand. OK, somebody was playing a joke on him, he thought wryly and he was starting to think it was Francis. How would a spoilt woman who spent her days between beauty parlours and the Caribbean even know what a crosshead screwdriver was? And she'd gone straight to it.

There was something funny going on here. Maybe the agency had sent the wrong person out?

She turned and caught the expression of perplexity on his face. 'What's the matter?'

'Nothing.' He frowned. No, he hadn't got the wrong person. How could he? She was Zoë Bernard, she'd told him so herself.

'Well, I give up on the belt for my dressing gown. I must have forgotten to pack it.' She shivered and hugged the flimsy silk material further around her slender frame.

'It's cold in here. You'd better get through to the other room before you get pneumonia.' He released the window and put down the tools to go over and give her a hand. 'I'll carry some of your things through for you.' He nodded towards the vanity case and the clothes she had left on the bed.

'Thanks, but I can manage.' For some reason his sudden concern and the warmth of his tone disconcerted her. She made to turn away from him. One moment she was keeping a polite distance, the next her foot had caught in the length of her gown and she was stumbling awkwardly.

Callum reached out instinctively and caught her.

The jolt knocked the air out of her lungs and she clung to him for a second. His body felt warm against hers. She could feel his hands burning through the light silk robe as he steadied her.

Slightly red in the face she pulled back from him, her heart pounding in mortification. 'Sorry!'

'That's OK.' His hands were still at her waist.

Her eyes collided with his.

Suddenly the feeling of breathlessness inside her wasn't down to embarrassment.

She felt his hands moving fractionally against the silk of

her nightwear, his thumbs caressing in a momentary whisper-softness just under her ribcage. She was aware he could feel her skin, taut and naked beneath the robe and a red-hot sweep of primal desire flooded through her.

Her eyes moved to the firm line of his lips. They were very close. If she just leaned against him a little more...

He noticed how her hair had dried into waves around her face. Her lips were a soft petal pink, her lashes dark against the creamy perfection of her skin. She was naturally beautiful...stunning in fact. The sensual feeling of her skin beneath the silk made him long to explore her, taste the satin of her skin, her lips. He blinked and moved back from her, horrified by what he had so nearly done.

'Sorry.' He murmured the word softly, his hands leaving the contact with her body as he stepped back from her.

She found it hard to think straight. Her chest felt tight, her skin hot.

'Lucky you didn't trip near the stairs, you could have really hurt yourself.'

For some reason the very gentleness of his tone disturbed her greatly, made her body long to go back into his arms.

'Yes.' She wrenched her eyes away from his and stepped past him to pick up her things.

'Here, allow me.' He reached to help but she had already bundled everything up.

'No, I'm fine.' She seemed to sing the words in a cheerful, breathy tone that didn't sound remotely like her. 'You fix the window. I'll see you downstairs later.'

Closing her bedroom door behind her, she leaned back against it. What on earth was wrong with her? She couldn't remember ever feeling so turned on and yet he had only held her for a moment. She wasn't even sure if the caress of his hands had been intentional or just a fleeting mistake.

She felt disorientated, her heart slamming against her ribs, her breasts taut and uncomfortable against her nightwear. Oh you are being ridiculous, Zoë, she scolded herself fiercely. 'You tripped, he caught you, there's nothing more to it than that. No chemistry, no hidden meaning. Sure, he's exceptionally good-looking, but that's no reason to melt as soon as he touches you. Get a grip.' She marched through to the other room, almost tripping again on the length of the gown and shut the door firmly and angrily behind her.

Across the corridor, Callum tried to put his attention back on the work in hand. But he couldn't get the memory of Zoë's firm and lovely body out of his mind. What had he been saying to himself earlier…? She wasn't his type? He frowned and tried to recapture the certainty of those feelings. All cashmere and silk, shallow and spoilt, not his type at all. 'Come on Francis, what's going on here?' he muttered dryly.

When he went downstairs a while later she was dressed in jeans and a red jumper. Her blonde hair was tied back from her face in a pony-tail.

How could she look so sexy in a pair of jeans, not a scrap of make-up on? he wondered.

'Breakfast?' she asked, spooning scrambled eggs out on toast for Alice and Kyle who were perfectly dressed and seated at the table.

'Just coffee and toast for me. Don't worry, I'll make it.' He ruffled Kyle's hair on the way past then sidestepped around Zoë as he went to switch on the kettle. He could smell her perfume, the same perfume that had lingered provocatively on the cotton sheets of her bed last night.

'We've named the lambs, Daddy,' Alice said, tucking in to her breakfast. 'The one with the black feet is called Skip, and the plain white one is called Skittle.'

Callum frowned. 'Whose idea was that?'

'Mine and Zoë's.' Alice smiled. 'Zoë said I can feed one and so can Kyle before we go to school.'

Callum noticed that Zoë had already made up two bottles. He poured his coffee and sat down at the kitchen table.

'Did you fix the window?' Zoë asked, sitting down opposite.

'No. I've secured it, but it's a bit draughty in there. Maybe you should stay in my room until I get a joiner in to look at it.'

'Maybe I should look at it for you.' She grinned.

He sipped his coffee and met her eyes across the table. 'So go on, then, tell me: how does a woman like you know anything about DIY?'

'What do you mean, a woman like me?' Her eyebrows lifted even more.

'I mean...' he searched for some polite words '...I mean...you look very sophisticated and stylish—'

'Thank you. But that doesn't mean I'm a helpless little female.'

Again their eyes caught across the table. Hell, he was attracted to her, Callum thought dazedly. This was never going to do. You promised Francis you would look after her, he told himself firmly. Keep your distance.

Zoë felt her senses stir as she remembered the intimacy of his body holding hers. She looked away, suddenly very self-conscious.

It was almost a relief when the children distracted their attention, arguing about which lamb they wanted to feed as they left the table.

'I'm not happy about this, Zoë,' Callum remarked in a low voice.

'About what?' She frowned as he indicated towards the children with a nod of his head.

'This is a working farm, not pets' corner at Whipsnade Zoo,' he murmured meaningfully. 'Christening them Skip and Skittle isn't a good idea.'

'Oh!' Zoë looked across at the two little bundles of white

fluff. 'Oh!' she reiterated in complete dismay before turning wide green eyes back on him. 'I see what you mean! Sorry, I forgot. I'm a vegetarian, you see.'

He shook his head in dismay. 'Hell, that's all I need, a veggie Sloane Ranger.'

'I beg your pardon?'

'Nothing.' He shook his head. 'Sorry, you're entitled to your principles.'

'Yes.' She nodded. 'I am. And I don't know where you got the idea that I'm some kind of Sloane Ranger, but I'm most certainly not.'

He smiled at the note of horror in her tone. 'I'm just starting to realise that,' he murmured softly.

There was a knock on the back door and, before anyone could get up to answer it, the door opened and a man of about thirty put his head around. 'Not interrupting am I?'

'Morning, Mark. Come on in,' Callum said cheerfully.

'Hello.' The man smiled at Zoë as he came into the room. 'I don't think we've met.'

'This is Zoë. She's helping out with the children for a few weeks,' Callum told him. 'Zoë, Mark.'

'I'm the local vet,' Mark told her, reaching to shake her hand.

Not bad looking either, Zoë thought. He was tall and well-built, with a decidedly mischievous glint in his dark eyes.

'I'm also his brother.' He nodded his head over towards Callum.

'I try to keep that quiet,' Callum murmured with a grin. 'It's not good for my image.'

'Watch it, or I won't drop everything and run out here at a moment's notice for you anymore.' Mark pulled out a chair and sat down at the table.

'Coffee or tea?' Zoë asked, breaking across their banter.

'Whatever is in the pot,' Mark said and watched as she got up to pour him a coffee.

He fixed his brother with a questioning look as she turned her back. 'Gorgeous,' he mouthed quietly. 'Where did you find her?'

'What did you say, Uncle Mark?' Alice asked innocently from beside him.

'Nothing, darling. How are you today?'

'Fine. Look, we've got two new baby lambs.'

'So I see.'

The conversation centred on the farm for a while as Zoë cleared away the breakfast dishes.

Then Callum glanced at his watch. 'Right. Time to leave for school. Get your stuff together, kids.'

'So, where do you hail from Zoë?' Mark asked as they were left alone together for a moment.

'London.'

'Really?' Mark looked surprised. 'You're a long way from home. Just fancied a change did you?'

'I'm only here for a few weeks,' Zoë said with a smile. 'I work for a temping agency.'

Mark frowned. 'In London?'

'Yes.'

'So why is Callum using a London agency?'

'A friend recommended us, apparently.'

'I see.' Mark hesitated. 'Maybe we could go out for a drink one night?' he asked. 'I'll show you some of our local hot spots before you leave.'

Callum overheard this as he returned to the room with his car keys. He frowned. The last thing he wanted was his brother asking Zoë out. 'If you want my advice, Zoë, you'll steer away from his hot spots. He'll be referring to his water-bed, or his sports car.'

'No, I am not,' Mark grinned at her and then winked so that Zoë wasn't sure if he was serious or not.

'Come on.' Callum moved impatiently towards the corridor and shouted for the children. 'You'll be late if you don't get down here.'

'So, how about it?' Mark asked as the children came thundering down the stairs.

'I'll take a rain check, Mark, but thanks for asking.'

'I'll catch you later when my big brother isn't around to inhibit you.' Mark grinned, not one bit perturbed by her refusal.

They left the house together and the children clambered into the back of the Land Rover as Zoë took the passenger seat beside Callum. With a wave at Mark, they were off down the long winding drive.

The sky was a brilliant blue, the fields were wet after a night of rain and they glinted in the sun, fresh and dazzlingly green, cut like a patchwork quilt by the pattern of stone walls that criss-crossed them.

The children were arguing in the back about who should have sat behind their father.

'Stop it, you two,' Callum said wearily. He slanted a look at Zoë, but she didn't appear to be listening. She looked as if she was miles away in thought. Thinking about her boyfriend? he wondered. She must be serious about him to turn down a date with Mark. Women usually fell over themselves for his younger brother.

They reached the road and the lake came into view. Its calm water reflected the purple mountains that rose steeply alongside it.

'That's Granny Ellen's house,' Kyle shrieked, making Zoë look around as they passed a stone cottage with smoke curling from the chimney.

Then they turned left over a bubbling beck and headed towards the village. Another half-hour and they were driving along the main street. It was a small community, Zoë noted. There was one main street with stone cottages, a picturesque Norman church, and a sub-postoffice. The school was at the far end of the village tucked away behind high walls. There was a lot of activity outside; cars were parked both sides of the road.

Callum was lucky enough to find a space by the main gates as another car pulled out.

'See you later, then,' he said as the children reached to kiss him before getting out.

Kyle hesitated before following Alice onto the pavement. 'Are you picking us up, Daddy?'

'No, Zoë will be here.'

Kyle frowned and slammed the door closed behind him.

'Do I detect a hint of frosty resentment from your son?' Zoë asked quietly.

'I'm afraid Kyle doesn't like change of any kind,' Callum answered, watching the two children as they went up the front steps of the school with a crowd of other friends. 'He'll be all right in a day or two.'

Zoë wasn't too sure about that.

An attractive, dark-haired woman of about Zoë's age, who was waving off her daughter, turned and saw Callum. 'Hello, stranger,' she said, sauntering over to talk to him.

Callum wound down the window. 'How are you doing, Sally?'

'Not so bad.' She slanted an inquisitive look over towards Zoë.

'Sally, this is Zoë. She's come up to help me with the children for a while.'

'Pleased to meet you,' Zoë said. She got a somewhat lukewarm smile in response.

'So, Callum, are you going to the Ashfield Ball next Saturday?' Sally continued as if Zoë wasn't there.

'I doubt it. I'm up to my eyes in work at the moment.'

'Oh, I know all that. But it's for a good cause, and we should all rally to support it.'

'Yeah, well, I'll buy a ticket whether I go or not—'

'That's not the point, Cal. They'll be relying on alcohol sales and the raffle.'

'I'll see how I'm fixed nearer the time.' Callum put the car into gear. 'Better be on my way. Nice seeing you, Sally.'

'Sally is the mother of one of Alice's friends,' Callum remarked as they drove away. But, for some reason, Zoë had the distinct impression that there was more to Sally than that.

'If you need anything, the village shop is around the next corner.' He slowed the vehicle for her to peer down a small side street. Then he accelerated away down the country roads towards home. 'But, if you want a bigger store, you'll have to drive into Windermere.'

'It must be about seventeen years since I was in Windermere,' Zoë reflected. 'It was our last family holiday before Mum died.'

'You'll find it hasn't changed much.'

'It's pretty though, isn't it? I was only little but I remember it quite clearly. Dad had a yacht on the lake. He was practising for the day when he'd take it out to sea.' She shook her head. 'He never quite got the hang of sailing.'

Thinking about her father, she felt sad for a moment. Maybe she should ring him, put him out of his misery and tell him she didn't intend to marry Matthew Devine.

'You can't have been very old when your mother died,' Callum said gently.

'I was eight.' She hesitated and then looked over at him. 'How long is it since you lost your wife?'

'Three years.' He changed gears. She watched him, noted the guarded expression that had crossed his handsome features.

'Sorry, I didn't mean to pry.'

'That's OK.'

'It's hard to let go of someone you loved, isn't it?' Zoë empathised.

He looked over at her then, noting the gentle expression in her eyes. 'You still miss your mother, don't you?'

'Yes, I do, even now after all these years.'

The car rattled over the cattle grid and, up ahead in the distance, Zoë could see the farmhouse: a large white building which sat in perfect harmony with the beauty of the surrounding fells. A small orchard sheltered the house on one side. The trees furled with fresh green buds ready to break into blossom. Behind, on the horizon, the mountains rose sharply, purple against the blue sky.

'I suppose a girl needs her mother,' Callum reflected.

'Yes, and so does an eight-year-old boy. I get the feeling that Kyle still misses his mother an awful lot.'

'He hardly remembers her…' Callum's voice trailed off. 'But, yes, I'm sure you're right and he does miss her.'

'You don't really like talking about this, do you?' Zoë asked, watching the dark expression that crossed the handsome features.

He glanced over at her. 'To be honest with you, it isn't something I usually talk about.'

She shrugged. 'Maybe you should. They say it's part of the healing process.'

His mouth twisted wryly. 'I'm all healed up.' He slanted a look of extreme irritation at her. 'Can we change the subject?'

'I'm sorry…it's none of my business. I shouldn't have said anything.'

'That's OK.' The fire of annoyance died as quickly as it had risen inside Callum. He glanced over at her again. There was a gentle sincerity about her that, perversely, made him regret asking her to drop the subject. He suddenly felt that anything she had to say would be worth listening to.

Up ahead a sheep wandered out into the road. Callum
slowed the car then brought it to a halt, glad of the excuse
to be able to train his attention on Zoë.

'I suppose Kyle just reminds me a little of myself at his
age. Like him, I felt very vulnerable, very insecure for a
long time.' She frowned then glanced up as if suddenly
aware that she had been speaking out loud.

'And was your dad able to talk to you about it?'

'He tried his best.' She smiled, but there was a tinge of
sadness in her eyes. 'He was devastated as well. He really
missed Mum. She was the love of his life. I think he coped
the way a lot of men cope. Bottled up his feelings to a large
extent and buried himself in his business.'

'And what did you do?' Callum asked quietly.

She shrugged. 'I learnt how to stand on my own two
feet.'

Callum frowned. Her naturalness, her lack of pretension,
struck him bodily.

'The road is clear.'

'Hmm?' It took a moment for him to focus on what she
was saying. His eyes moved over the beauty of her features,
the brightness of her eyes. He remembered how good she
had felt to hold close.

'I said, the road is clear.'

'Yes, so it is.' He pulled his gaze away from her. She
was too captivating by far. Maybe this was the problem.
Perhaps he was so sensually attracted to her that it was
blinding his judgement of her character. After all, Francis
had to be telling the truth about her…didn't he? Otherwise
why would he have sent her up here?

She looked out again at the scenery as he put the car in
gear and moved forward.

'So, how are things between you and your father these
days?' he asked gently.

'They are OK.' She glossed over the subject, not wanting

to stir any deeper into that particular cauldron. She had just wanted to let Callum know that she understood how difficult things were for him.

Callum pulled the car around the back of the house and wished they hadn't arrived back so soon. There was so much more he wanted to find out about Zoë.

'Your brother is still here by the looks of things,' Zoë said as she noticed his car was parked next to hers.

'Must be some complication with the livestock,' Callum said, frowning. 'Unless he's just hanging around for another shot at asking you out. My brother isn't used to rejection. It has to be a first for him.'

Zoë glanced at him. She reckoned she could apply that statement equally to the two brothers. They were both very good-looking. Callum had the edge though, she thought. He was taller, broader, had the more rugged athletic look about him.

They headed into the farmhouse. Callum picked up a pair of wellingtons from behind the kitchen door and sat down to put them on. 'The children get out of school at three-thirty. You'll find your way back to the school OK?' he asked.

'Of course I will.' Indignation shone from the bright green eyes. 'I found my way up here, didn't I?'

He smiled at that. 'OK. But you had better use my four-wheel drive while you are here.' He straightened and tossed his keys down on the pine table. 'The roads can be treacherous at this time of year. It will be safer than that sports car of yours. And don't forget to feed the twins.' He nodded towards the lambs that were bleating balefully from the pen that he had set up to hold them beside the Rayburn.

'You mean Skip and Skittle?' she said with a teasing gleam in her eye.

'You know what I mean,' he answered wryly.

He was about to go when the phone rang in the hall. He

frowned. 'Will you answer that for me, Zoë, please? I don't want to walk through the kitchen in these boots.'

She nodded and hurried out to pick it up. She expected someone to ask for Callum. It was a surprise therefore to hear her flatmate's voice. 'Oh, Zoë, I'm glad you've answered the phone.' Honey sounded relieved. 'Listen, how do you work the washing machine? I've got an audition for a show this afternoon and I've forgotten to wash my lucky leotard.'

Zoë grinned. Honey was the most superstitious person she had ever met. 'Hold on a moment and I'll talk you through it.' She covered the phone and called to Callum. 'It's OK, it's for me,' she said before turning her attention back to Honey. Their washing machine had become notoriously temperamental over these last few weeks. Getting it to work involved a lot of twiddling of the knobs and a firm kick. They should have replaced it last time it broke down, Zoë supposed. But, at the time, they had both been strapped for cash.

Callum frowned. Francis's plan seemed to be backfiring somewhat. Instead of distancing her from Mr Unsuitable, she seemed to be on the phone morning, noon and night to him. He was about to shout out that, instead of chatting to her boyfriend, he'd appreciate some work being done around here, then closed his mouth and thought better of it.

Callum found his brother up in the top pasture. He stopped work as Callum joined him. 'So, what's the low-down on the delectable Zoë?' he asked immediately.

'There is no low-down,' Callum replied abruptly.

'Are you interested in her?' Mark asked. Then his face cleared and he held up his hands. 'Wow, Cal, that's great! I'm sorry, I didn't realise, otherwise I never would have asked her out—'

'I am not interested in her. But I'd appreciate it if you'd keep your distance just the same.'

'Why?'

'She's an employee. I don't want any complications.'

Mark shook his head. 'Sorry, Brother, but that's not a good enough reason for me to keep away. She's simply gorgeous.'

Callum found himself remembering how she had looked in the shower this morning. He wished he could disagree with Mark. But, unfortunately, he couldn't.

'So, tell me,' Mark continued, 'which friend recommended this London temping agency to you?'

'Just leave it,' Callum murmured. 'It's no one you know.'

# CHAPTER FOUR

THE children had just finished their homework and were going to watch TV before bed when there was a knock at the back door and an older woman stepped into the room.

'Grandma!' They both gave squeals of delight as they raced over to greet her.

'Hello, darlings. Just thought I'd pop over and see how you are.' She gave them both a hug, and then glanced over at Zoë.

'I'm Ellen. You must be Zoë.'

'Yes.' Zoë reached to shake hands. She seemed a pleasant woman, well-groomed with sleek white hair combed back from a face that had an arresting bone structure and sherry-brown eyes.

'I hope these children are behaving for you?'

Something about the glint in Ellen's eyes as she asked that question made Zoë smile. 'They've been very good.'

'I'm pleased to hear it.' The woman took off her coat and hung it up behind the door.

'Callum still out working, I take it?'

Zoë nodded.

'Lambing is a difficult time for him,' Ellen murmured as she sat down at the table.

She accepted Zoë's offer of a cup of tea and, for a while, they all sat chatting around the kitchen table. Then it was time for the children to go to bed.

Ellen went up with them as Zoë finished tidying the kitchen.

'You seem to have made a hit,' Ellen said when she returned.

'I don't know about that,' Zoë laughed. 'Kyle had poetry for his homework tonight and I don't think he was too pleased when I told him he had to practise it again.'

'Actually, he seems happy.' The woman's eyes moved over Zoë in a thoughtful manner. 'Well, I had better get off. I don't like to be out too late these nights.'

As Ellen started to walk towards the kitchen door, a look of pain crossed her face. 'I'm OK,' she said immediately as she saw the look of concern on Zoë's face. 'It's just my arthritis,' she explained. 'It's been very painful just recently.'

Zoë nodded.

'Don't mention it to Callum, though,' the woman told her anxiously. 'If he knew I wasn't well he'd insist on my taking things easy all the time, and I don't really want to. I was the one who insisted on taking hold of the reins for him when Helen died.'

'Well, you should take the opportunity while I'm here to get some rest,' Zoë said firmly.

'I intend to.' Ellen sighed. 'To be honest with you Zoë, when Callum told me you were coming it was like an answer to a prayer.'

'I don't think I've ever been described as that before.' Zoë grinned. 'Callum must have realised you needed a rest.'

'That's the funny thing.' Ellen frowned. 'I thought I'd done so well hiding just how bad I was from him. Then, all of a sudden, he sprung it on me that you were coming for a few weeks.'

'Maybe Mark noticed something.'

Ellen shook her head. 'Anyway, the important thing is that Callum has you. I can put my feet up without worrying.'

\* \* \*

Ellen had gone and the tea things tidied away when Callum arrived home a while later.

He stepped into the warmth of the kitchen and noticed how clean and orderly everything was. Even when Millie was here, the place didn't look as good as this. There was also a wonderful smell of cooking coming from the oven.

He walked across the kitchen and through to the lounge. The rest of the house seemed similarly clean and tidy: the cushions plumped up on the settee, the fire blazing brightly in the grate.

He wandered upstairs to check on the children. They were both fast asleep.

He'd have a shower and then eat, he decided. He felt very tired.

He opened the door to his bedroom and there was Zoë sprawled out on his bed, fast asleep. For a moment, he stared at her, wondering what she was doing there. Then he remembered that they had swapped rooms.

She was wearing a long red skirt and a black top, and her blonde hair was loose over the covers in a golden halo around her face. Something stirred inside him, something deep and primal. He would have liked to go across and take her into his arms, kiss the sensuous curve of her lips. It was a long time since he'd come home to a beautiful woman in his bed.

He started to back out of the door and her dark eyelashes flickered open. 'Sorry, I forgot you were in here,' he said apologetically.

'That's OK.' She stretched and looked at the clock. 'I only lay down for a moment and, the next thing, I was asleep. It must have been all the travelling yesterday and then an early morning.' He got a glimpse of long shapely legs as she swung them over the side of the bed.

'Have you eaten?' she asked.

'No, I thought I'd shower first. Do you mind if I take some clothes out of my wardrobe?'

'Go ahead.' She stood up. 'I'll go downstairs and give you some space.'

When he returned downstairs after showering and changing she was in the kitchen.

'There's a nice smell in here,' he remarked. 'What is it?'

'One of my specialities.'

'What? Bean casserole?' He grinned and pulled a disdainful face. 'You're not trying to turn the children into veggies, are you?'

'And what is wrong with being a vegetarian?' she asked, fixing him with a teasing look. 'Do you want to try some?'

'Not really.'

'But I left some especially for you.'

He watched as she took a casserole dish out of the oven.

'That's very good of you,' he said, taken aback. 'But I don't expect you to have a meal ready for me when I come in. It's just the children I'm concerned with.'

She shrugged. 'It's no trouble. It's just what was left over from their meal anyway.'

She turned away to fill the kettle as he picked up the plate of food she had dished up for him.

'This isn't a vegetarian meal.'

She looked around at him. 'I never said it was. You jumped to that conclusion on your own.'

'Yes, I suppose I did.' He sat down at the table and tried a few mouthfuls. 'It's very good.'

'You know, there really is no need to sound so surprised. I am a qualified chef. It is in my references.'

'But what is written in a reference isn't necessarily strictly accurate, is it?' he said, grinning over at her.

'So, why did you employ me then?' she asked suddenly.

He almost choked on his food.

'There must have been other candidates for the job.

Martin probably sent you a selection of CVs from the agency to sift through.'

'No. He didn't.' That, at least, was the truth. 'They just sent yours.'

She frowned.

'Anyway, Martin highly recommended you.' Callum tried to diffuse the atmosphere. 'And, if this meal is anything to go by, I know why.'

He finished eating and took his plate to the dishwasher. 'Where did you learn to cook like that anyway?' he asked.

She hesitated. She could have told him that she had learnt at a Swiss finishing-school, but it sounded a bit pretentious. 'I love cooking. It's one of my passions, along with eating.'

His eye flicked over her slender figure. 'For someone who likes to eat, there isn't much of you,' he remarked.

'I work out a lot at my local gym.'

Remembering the slender curves of her figure as he'd held her this morning, Callum could well believe that.

'So, how was your day?' He changed the subject abruptly. 'Any problems?'

'Not really.'

For a moment, he thought that she was going to leave the room and go back upstairs. He didn't want that. What he really wanted was to get to know her, try and find out what was fact and what was fiction from what Francis Bernard had told him about his daughter.

'Would you like a glass of wine?' he asked her on impulse.

She looked around, surprised by the offer. 'Yes, I would, thanks.'

He took out a bottle of Chablis from the fridge.

She watched him as he uncorked the bottle. He was wearing a fawn pair of chinos and a ribbed beige jumper. The light colours suited his dark colouring.

'Let's make ourselves more comfortable in the lounge,

shall we?' Without waiting for her reply, he turned to lead the way through into the other room.

The fire was burning brightly in the grate and two side lamps lit the room, giving it an intimate, cosy glow. Zoë sat down in the chair closest to the fire and curled her feet up beneath her.

'You must be tired,' she said, looking across at him as he sat down on the settee immediately opposite to her.

'I am, it's a hectic time of the year.' He poured out two glasses of wine and passed one across to her, leaving the bottle between them on the table. 'But I'm glad you're here to help me through it.'

'Even though I'm a veggie Sloane Ranger?' she teased softly.

'If I've been a bit wary about you, Zoë, I'm sorry.' He sat back in the settee. 'But, you know, I've never had anyone in to look after the children that I don't know. Since Helen died it's either been my mother, or Millie. And I've known Millie for years. The children are my most treasured possession, and you are—'

'Something of an unknown entity?' Zoë finished for him. 'I can understand that.'

He smiled at her. 'Thanks.'

'What for?'

'For understanding what I was trying to say…and for trying to talk to me about Kyle this morning. I'm sorry if I was a bit abrupt.'

'I was just trying to help.'

'I know you were,' His eyes held hers. 'You seem to be a woman of many hidden talents and depths.'

'Well, I can cook,' she murmured, feeling a little self-conscious.

'Yes.' He smiled. 'And I'm greatly relieved to know that the children won't be living on nut cutlets for the next few weeks.'

She laughed. 'I'm not promising I won't give then an occasional vegetarian meal.'

'I can live with that.'

There was a moment's silence. She had a lovely laugh, Callum reflected, warm and infectious, and he liked the way it reached her eyes, making them sparkle and dance with merriment. He pulled himself up. 'How were the children today?' he asked, trying to sound brisk and businesslike.

Zoë smiled. 'Kyle was in a mood when he came out of school because he got detention at break time. But he soon cheered up.'

'What had he done?'

Zoë suppressed a smile. 'He let the school pet mouse out in the classroom. It caused uproar apparently.'

'I can imagine,' Callum murmured. 'I don't know where he gets it from.'

'I suppose you were always a model pupil?' Zoë sipped her wine and looked at him over the rim of her glass.

'Always.' His eyes held a teasing light as they met hers. 'What about you?'

'Perfect in every way.' She nodded, a glint of mischief in her green eyes. 'Except for when I was nearly expelled.'

Callum's eyebrows rose. 'What did you do?'

She paused and then grinned. 'I'll tell you but you have to promise not to hold it against me. I am a very trustworthy person these days.'

He watched the way the firelight played over her smooth creamy skin, and noted the earnest expression in her eyes. She looked very young, almost like a teenager with that long flowing hair and pouting soft lips. 'So, go on, tell me what happened.'

'Dad sent me to a boarding school and I hated it. So, I set about getting myself liberated. I did everything I could possibly think of to get out of there. But they just kept giving me warnings.' She wrinkled her nose. 'So, I organised a mass exodus of the girls at lights out. We sneaked out and went down to the local village hop.'

'How old were you?'

'Thirteen. We just danced and talked to some of the local boys. It was innocent, really. We didn't drink or anything. I have to own up to smoking one cigarette though, which made me feel very sick.' She grinned. 'Anyway, one of the girls from another dormitory had snitched on us and Mr Hawkins, that was the headmaster, followed us down to the hall.' She sighed. 'But he still didn't expel me.'

It sounded as if her father had endured a rough time of it, Callum thought with a certain amount of sympathy for the man. 'If you hated the school so much, why didn't you just ask your dad if you could leave?'

'I did.' Zoë took another sip of her wine. 'I begged him to let me come home. But he just told me to toughen up. That it was good for me. I suppose, in all fairness to him, he was busy and he thought that at least I was being looked after at boarding school.' She frowned for a moment as she thought about it.

'So what happened?' Callum asked.

'Oh, I was in big trouble.' Zoë rolled her green eyes expressively and Callum laughed.

'And were you ever expelled?'

'No. I decided to conform after that and became a model pupil. Unfortunately I had to serve my full sentence there.'

'You make it sound like jail.'

'That's what it felt like,' she said quietly. 'They had a very strict regime. It was austere and formal to the point of lacking any human compassion. I was very unhappy, very homesick.'

'Surely if you had tried talking with your father he would have relented, at least changed the school.'

'You don't know my father,' Zoë said with a wry smile.

'As I was trying to explain this morning, he's not the easiest person to talk to.'

Callum moved uncomfortably in his seat.

'And, anyway, the school was very expensive and had a very good reputation for turning out young ladies of quality.' She wrinkled her nose. 'My father kept saying, "You're lucky to go there, and these school days are the happiest years of your life, you just don't realise it."' She shuddered. 'And when he said that, I really used to get depressed.'

'We all say that to kids, though, don't we?' Callum said with a smile. 'We just mean that school days are a relatively carefree time.'

'Not for some children they're not,' Zoë said firmly. She finished her wine.

'Have you got any brothers or sisters?' he asked.

'No. Mum couldn't have any more children and, after she died, Dad never married again, I'm sorry to say.'

'You'd have liked him to remarry?'

'I think it would have been good for him to share his life with someone again. After Mum, he focused his whole life on business and, although he's been very successful, I think he's lonely.'

'At least he had one great love in his life,' Callum said reflectively. 'And he's got you.'

Zoë inclined her head and wondered if that was how Callum felt about his own situation. 'But I don't think Mum would have wanted him to be alone for ever.'

'I don't think Helen would want me to be alone for ever either,' Callum murmured. 'But I suppose you're lucky if you find happiness a second time.'

'Yes…I suppose so.'

His eyes met with hers and, for some reason, she felt as if she was holding her breath for a moment.

Callum was the first to look away. 'Sorry…your glass is empty,' he said, reaching for the bottle of wine.

She hesitated and then shook her head. 'I'd better not have another one.'

She wondered if the drink was affecting her, because she had felt a bit light-headed when Callum had looked at her. It had been a strange sensation.

Callum topped up his own glass and tried to concentrate on what they had been talking about before he had looked into her eyes.

'And is your father still as successful?' he probed, endeavouring to sound nonchalant.

'Yes, more than ever.'

'That must be nice.'

'Well, I'd be lying if I didn't say it had its moments. For instance, the car I'm driving was a twenty-first birthday present.'

There! Proof. She liked the money and the lifestyle. But so what? He frowned to himself. Wouldn't anybody?

'But money isn't everything, Callum.' She met his eyes steadily. 'I know that probably sounds a bit clichéd, but it's true. Dad used to send me on the most fabulous holidays when I was at school and at college. It was kind of him, but he did it because he wouldn't be home, so he thought if he bought expensive jet-setting trips and got a minder for me, I'd be happy. Truth was, I would have much preferred to spend the time with him. There are some things you can't make right just by throwing money at it. Money couldn't save Mum when she was sick…and it can't buy self-respect…especially if you haven't earned it yourself. That's why I don't accept gifts from my father anymore. It upsets him. He thinks I'm being difficult.' She shrugged. 'But there comes a time in everyone's life when they have to be independent, and I can't do that if Dad is continually wanting to take over, give me things, make things right…

However well-intentioned his motives, I have to make my own way in life.'

'Do you think your mother's death gave you a more realistic perception of life?' Callum suggested gently.

'Yes, I do.' She looked over at him, for some reason grateful that he understood. 'It's certainly what has driven me to learn all the skills I have, so I can stand on my own...' She trailed off, suddenly feeling self-conscious. 'Sorry, I always seemed to be talking about my father...don't I?'

Probably because I keep leading her in that direction, Callum thought guiltily.

'Anyway...' her voice lightened '...we've talked enough about me, don't you think?'

'Not really.' He smiled. 'I am very interested.'

He had gorgeous dark eyes, she found herself thinking. In fact, Callum Langston was a bit too good-looking for comfort. With difficulty, she pulled her thoughts away from that direction.

'Even so, I think it's only reasonable that you should tell me your most wicked moment at school. After all, I have made my confession.'

'I told you, I was a model pupil.' He grinned.

'Bet if I asked Mark he'd tell me different.'

'He'd probably tell you about the time I put maggots in the teacher's desk.'

'You didn't?' Zoë's eyes widened. 'That's worse than anything I ever did. Your poor teacher.'

He smiled. 'It was a vicious lie; it wasn't me. Probably it was Mark.'

'Classic case of guilt; blame it on the little brother.' Zoë grinned. 'Have you always lived in Cumbria?'

'No. I was originally from Cheshire. I came to the Lakes for a holiday and I never went home...well, except to sell up.' His lips twisted ruefully. 'I was pretty impulsive in those days.'

'I take it you met your wife here and that was what decided you?'

He looked away from her. 'Yes, it was.' He put his glass down on the table. 'Would you like a coffee?'

'No, thanks. Maybe I will have just half a glass of wine instead.' She reached forward to pick up the bottle at the same time as he did. Their hands met on the cool glass. He looked up at her and, for a moment, they just stared into each other's eyes. A strong surge of desire flared suddenly inside Zoë. It was the most extraordinary feeling, coming so out of the blue. She pulled away. 'Sorry.'

'That's OK. Allow me.' He lifted the bottle and refilled her glass.

She wondered if he had noticed how his touch affected her. How it had affected her this morning when she had fallen into his arms. The notion that he had was deeply embarrassing. He was her employer for heaven's sakes!

'I'm glad we're getting this chance to relax together, get to know one another better,' he said softly.

She looked over at him, uncertainty in her eyes.

'It's good to know that the children are with someone I can trust.'

'Oh…yes.' Why did she feel disappointed? Why had she hoped he had wanted to know her for more personal reasons?

She toyed with the glass of wine for a moment.

'I suppose things seem very quiet and boring for you here, after London,' he remarked.

She shook her head. 'Not at all.'

'What do you do down there when you're not working?'

She shrugged. 'Usual things, go for a drink, or to the theatre, or out for a meal. And I enjoy painting.'

'Portraits?'

'No, mostly landscapes.'

'Well, that's one thing we have a lot of here.' He smiled.

When he smiled at her like that she could almost forget that his interest in her was purely because she was in charge of his children. She liked Callum Langston a lot, she thought suddenly.

She finished her wine and put down the glass. 'Well, I suppose I'd better turn in.' She put her feet back down on the floor. 'Oh…before I forget. Kyle has a school concert tomorrow at six-thirty. He really wants you to come.'

Callum raked a hand through his hair.

'It's important to him, Callum,' she told him softly before he could answer.

Callum's eyes moved over the serious expression in her eyes and he nodded. 'I will be there,' he assured her. 'But why do they make these things so darn early?'

'Probably because the children have to get to bed darn early,' she suggested with a twinkle of amusement in her eye.

He smiled. He liked the fact that she knew the concert was important to Kyle. He liked the humorous glint in her beautiful eyes. In fact, he was starting to like everything about her.

She glanced at her watch. 'Is it all right if I use the phone?'

Callum frowned, then quickly pulled himself up. 'Yes, of course.'

Must be a serious relationship if she was ringing her boyfriend again, he thought as he watched her go through to the hallway. For some reason he found he didn't like that idea. Maybe it was because her father had told him the guy was a con man and, behind that very confident exterior, he sensed that Zoë had a vulnerable quality.

He could hear her dialling. Here we go again, he thought, wondering if he should turn on the TV and give her some

privacy. He didn't move. There was a part of him that was
deeply curious. Just when he thought he had her weighed
up, she'd look at him with those fascinating green eyes and
say something that completely bowled him over.

The way she had spoken about her father's money, for
instance. He could completely understand where she was
coming from. He liked that gutsy, independent streak.
Francis was wrong about his daughter. Was he also wrong
about the guy she was dating?

He shouldn't have become involved with Francis's wild
scheme, he told himself guiltily. But he'd known Francis
for a long time and the man had seemed genuinely concerned about his daughter. What was it he had said?
'Matthew Devine is a small-time crook and a confidence
trickster—'

Would Francis have gone to the trouble of getting his
daughter up here if he wasn't out of his mind with worry?
It had to be very difficult for him, especially as he wasn't
a well man.

He would do this favour for Francis and keep her busy
while he got rid of Mr Unsuitable. And he wouldn't feel
guilty about it, he told himself firmly. Zoë was being paid
damn good money to keep house for him and, if she hadn't
wanted the job, she shouldn't have come here.

But the sense of unease continued.

Out in the hallway, Zoë was ringing her father with a
feeling of trepidation. She wasn't going to back down; she
needed to be able to live her own life. But she didn't like
this silence between them. Her conversation with Callum
had made her think about her father again. Yes, he was too
tough sometimes, too overbearing, but he did love her,
didn't he?

The phone rang and rang and then the answering machine clicked in. Zoë put the phone down and glanced at

her watch. It was almost eleven. Where was he? she wondered.

She wandered back through to the lounge.

'No answer?' Callum enquired idly.

'No.' Zoë wondered if she should have left a message.

She seemed upset. Callum frowned. How upset would
she be when she got back to London and discovered that
Mr Unsuitable had been bought off?

'I wouldn't worry about it. He's probably out having a
pint.'

'And what makes you think I was ringing a man?' Zoë
slanted a light-hearted look over at him.

'Just a shot in the dark.' He smiled. 'But you were,
weren't you?'

'Yes. But no ordinary man—'

A cry from upstairs interrupted them. 'Sounds like one
of the children. Shall I go?'

'No. I'll see to it.' Callum hurried away up the stairs.

It was Kyle. He was having a nightmare and was crying
in his sleep. Callum soothed him, wiping his face, cradling
him in his arms for a while until the child went back into
a restful sleep again.

Zoë paused on her way past the open door and watched
Callum's tenderness with the child. He was warm and loving towards his children. She liked that.

'Is he OK?' she whispered as he turned to come out of
the room.

He nodded. 'Just a bad dream.'

She smiled. 'Well, goodnight, then.'

''Night.'

As she opened the door into her bedroom, he followed
her onto the landing. 'Zoë?'

'Yes?' She looked around at him.

Hell, he wished she wouldn't look at him like that, those

wide, come-to-bed eyes made it hard for him to concentrate.

'I was wondering when you last fed the lambs?'

'Just after dinner.'

'OK.' He smiled. 'Well, goodnight, see you in the morning.'

She smiled. 'See you in the morning.'

Callum turned towards the spare bedroom. He stripped off his clothes in the dark and got straight into bed. Zoë's perfume still lingered on the sheets. It was somehow very provocative.

He'd been on the verge of asking her out. Heavens knows what had possessed him. She had a boyfriend, she was only here for a few weeks... He had lied to her about the job; he was in cahoots with her father. He ran through the list of reasons for not getting involved and then tried to turn his mind away from Zoë. But the impish sparkle in her green eyes lingered on his mind's image just as her perfume did on the sheets. He turned over restlessly.

He wondered if the fact that she was disturbing him with that sensual body and those big eyes was down to the fact that he hadn't gone out on a date for a long time.

His thoughts turned to Helen. Beautiful Helen, with her laughing eyes, so full of life. What would she have advised him to do?

# CHAPTER FIVE

THE house was empty when Callum returned to it the next evening. Obviously, Zoë had already left for the school concert. He'd asked her to take the Land Rover and go ahead without him if he was a bit late, promising to catch her up later.

He glanced at the clock. He must have only just missed her.

Hurriedly he made his way through the kitchen and out into the hall. The answering machine was flashing. He turned up the volume and pressed play as he dashed up the stairs. He really didn't have time to listen to messages if he wanted to shower, change, and get to the school hall on time.

A man's voice saying Zoë's name made him pause on the landing.

'Darling,' it drawled, 'it's Matthew. Everything is set for the fifteenth. Will you ring me when you get in? And, by the way, your father has been around to see me. I'd like to talk to you about it.'

Callum's hand froze as he started to pull his shirt off. Hell! What was this Matthew bloke going to tell her? Your father is trying to buy me off? Your father has sent you on a wild goose chase just to get me out of your life? No, it wouldn't be the latter. Francis was a shrewd man; he wouldn't be so stupid as to let that piece of information slip, would he? And what was set for the fifteenth? he wondered.

He tore off the rest of his clothes and hastily got into the shower. He'd ring Francis later and get the facts. But he'd no time now. He couldn't be late for Kyle.

As he changed into a pair of green chinos and a fleece, he debated whether he should press 'save' on the machine. He really should. He had no right to interfere in Zoë's private life.

He hurried back down the stairs. He noticed suddenly that there were fresh flowers in the lounge and on the hall table. Zoë had cut lilac from the orchard and placed it in crystal vases. The soft blooms had only recently unfurled from the delicate green shoots. The evocative perfume invaded his mind for a moment.

There hadn't been flowers in the house for a long time. Helen had been the last person to pick the lilac blossom and put them in these vases. She had always liked the house filled with fresh flowers. If he closed his eyes he could see her arranging them, smiling at him. 'There,' she'd say softly, 'spring is here, better times around the corner.'

Callum glanced at the answering machine, his hand paused over the save button. Then, for some reason, he pressed erase.

The school hall smelt of polish and candle wax. Hardback chairs had been positioned in rows in front of the small stage and the windows were lit with the inviting flicker of candles that were lined up along the sills.

Once Kyle was ensconced back stage, Zoë found some spare seats a few rows from the front and led Alice over to them. She hoped Callum wouldn't be long because, already, the hall was starting to fill up.

'We'll keep a place for Daddy,' she told Alice as she put her handbag on the empty seat next to her. Then she helped the child to take her wet raincoat off.

'Excuse me?' A female voice made Zoë turn around. It took a few moments before she recognised the person standing in the aisle as the woman Callum had introduced her to outside the school.

'Oh, hello.' Zoë acknowledged her with a smile. She looked very attractive in a long black coat and a grey trouser suit, her dark hair swinging silkily as she moved. 'Sally, isn't it?'

'Yes. Just wondered if there was anyone sitting in that chair next to you?'

'I'm reserving it for Callum,' Zoë explained. 'Hopefully he'll be along in a moment.'

The woman nodded and took the seat on the other side of the empty chair. 'How are you settling in?' she asked Zoë. 'Not finding it too boring up here after London?'

'I'm settling in very well, thank you,' Zoë replied. 'How did you know I was from London?'

'Callum must have mentioned it.' Sally took off her coat and put it carefully over the back of her chair. 'You're working late tonight, aren't you?'

'I wouldn't really class this as work,' Zoë said with a shrug. 'I'm quite looking forward to the performance.'

Sally raised her eyebrows. 'You must be a sucker for punishment. I certainly wouldn't be here only Clara—that's my eldest daughter—insisted. I find these things rather tedious.' She crossed her arms and fixed her with a direct look. 'So, tell me, Zoë, are you planning to stay up here for long?' she asked brusquely.

Zoë suddenly felt as if she was being interrogated but, before she could answer, Alice bent her head to look over at the other woman. 'I hope Zoë stays a very long time,' she said firmly.

'How sweet,' Sally murmured.

Zoë looked at the little girl. 'Thank you, Alice, that's a very nice thing to say.'

The lights began to dim; the room was only lit by candlelight now. The concert was about to start. Zoë looked around towards the door. Where was Callum?

As if on cue, the door opened and he walked in just as the curtain went up. Zoë raised her hand and gave a wave so that he would see them.

'Sorry,' Callum whispered as he squeezed past Sally to take his seat.

'I was starting to worry that you wouldn't make it,' Zoë whispered.

'So was I.' He grinned at her. 'Thanks for covering for me.'

Hell, but he was attractive, Zoë thought as she looked into his eyes.

She turned her attention to the stage and tried to forget how close he was. But, in reality, she was very conscious of his long legs resting slightly against hers in the confined space, the subtle tang of his aftershave, deliciously warm and somehow arousing.

'Welcome to our celebration of spring,' a child was saying in a very stilted and self-conscious voice.

Zoë smiled as Kyle stepped forward. 'A time of new beginnings and warmer days,' he said moving his hands in a way the teacher must have taught him to do.

Then the pianist struck up and the children sang 'All Things Bright And Beautiful' in stirring chorus. Kyle's face was wreathed in smiles as he saw his father and he seemed to be singing loudest of all.

After the song, a few of the children took turns going up to the podium to read verses of poetry.

Kyle read Wordsworth's 'Daffodils'. He stumbled a little midway through and Zoë murmured the line for him, willing him to get it right, which he did. Then, amid rapturous applause, the curtain went down for the interval.

'You seem to know Wordsworth rather well.' Callum grinned, turning to look at Zoë.

'I suppose everyone does. But it's been Kyle's homework for the last two nights so, really, I should know it backwards by now.'

'Daddy?' Alice reached across Zoë to tug at her father's sleeve. 'Do you like my hair?' she asked, turning so that he could see the woven plaits at the back.

'Beautiful, darling,' Callum said.

'Zoë did it for me before we came out,' Alice said happily. 'She did Barbie's hair as well. Look.' The child passed her doll over for inspection.

As Callum looked at the doll, Zoë suddenly felt self-conscious and hot. He probably thought that she shouldn't be wasting time on such trivialities. The feeling was made worse as Sally leaned over towards Callum to look at the doll as well.

'That's very good, Zoë,' she said with a patronising smile. 'You lost your way, you should have been a hairdresser.'

Zoë forced herself to smile back at the woman. 'Oh, I can turn my hand to most things,' she said with bright confidence.

'Your housekeeper seems quite a find, Callum. You must tell me all about this agency in London. I could do with getting someone like Zoë myself.'

Callum handed the doll back to Alice and made no reply to that.

The lights dimmed again and the curtain rose. Zoë could hear Sally's voice whispering something to Callum. She slanted a look sideways and could see the woman's head resting very close to his. For some reason this irritated her.

None of your business, Zoë, she kept telling herself, but couldn't help casting a quick glance sideways again. Not only was Sally leaning over whispering in his ear, but she was also flaunting a considerable amount of cleavage in the process.

Zoë focused on Kyle and refused to be sidetracked further. But, despite what she was telling herself, all her senses seemed tuned in to what was happening beside her.

Sally was keeping up some kind of a running commentary. Her voice was so low and husky that Zoë couldn't make out what she was saying, but it was a damn distraction.

As the children took their final bow and the curtain came down for the last time to terrific applause, Kyle's teacher announced that refreshments were being served in the adjacent hall.

'Why don't you come across to my house for a drink instead?' Sally asked Callum as he helped her on with her coat.

'I can't, Sally. I didn't drive here; one of the farm labourers dropped me off on his way home. So I'll have to go back with Zoë and the children.'

Sally looked up at him coyly from beneath dark lashes. 'Well, maybe another evening, then?'

'Yes, I'll look forward to it.'

Zoë buttoned up Alice's coat for her and tried not to listen in to their conversation. Was Sally single? Zoë wondered. If body language was anything to go by, hers seemed to be screaming availability.

'Shall we go across to the hall and have a cup of tea?' Callum suggested. 'How about it, Zoë?'

'Would you mind if I didn't?' Zoë smiled and couldn't help noticing the look of annoyance on Sally's face. She had obviously been hoping it would be a chance to get Callum to herself for a moment. 'I'm a bit tired.' Plus she really didn't fancy playing gooseberry. She'd had enough of Sally's fluttering eyelashes and heaving bosom for one evening.

'No, I don't mind at all.' Callum shrugged.

They waited for the children to come from backstage.

Kyle arrived first, his eyes shining with excitement as he came running over towards his father. 'What did you think, Dad?'

'I thought you were brilliant,' Callum said enthusiastically.

Sally's daughter sauntered towards them in a more lady-like fashion. She was very like her mother, Zoë thought, same dark straight hair, same cool look in her eyes as if she was slightly bored with life.

'You were very good in the concert,' Zoë said to her as they made their way outside.

'Yes, I know,' Clara replied nonchalantly. 'I'm thinking about a career on the stage.'

She sounded like an eight-year-old going on eighteen, Zoë thought wryly.

'Clara is naturally gifted at most things,' Sally said. 'She is incredibly academic, a straight A student. A bit like I was at her age.'

'I'm always top in my class,' Clara agreed and then glanced almost gleefully at Kyle. 'And Kyle's always bottom.'

'Well, it's not where you start it's where you finish,' Zoë replied swiftly. She put an arm on Kyle's shoulder. 'Isn't that right, Kyle?'

Kyle didn't reply. He looked downcast.

Callum noted the protective way Zoë had sprung to Kyle's defence. His gaze took in the hand that rested lightly, unobtrusively on his son's shoulder.

It was raining outside. They paused in the front entrance as Zoë rooted in her handbag for the car keys. Sally pulled Callum quietly to one side to say something to him.

Zoë couldn't hear what it was because the stream of people leaving the hall separated them. She could see that Sally had a hand resting proprietorially on Callum's leather jacket. And she was looking up into his eyes with a serious, absorbed interest. They made an attractive couple, she thought, and then frowned at the idea. No, Sally wasn't his type. She was attractive, sensual but cool. He deserved someone a bit… She halted her opinion in mid flow. What was she doing? Callum's personal life was nothing to do with her.

'Kyle, button up your coat please.' Zoë switched her attention to the children. 'You'll get soaked out there.'

'I'm all right,' Kyle said stubbornly.

Zoë crouched down to fasten it up for him. 'What is Sally saying to my dad?' Kyle asked her.

'I don't know, Kyle. But it will probably be something to do with school business,' Zoë said dismissively, although it looked like business of a more personal nature to her.

'I think he's asking my mum out on a date,' Clara said suddenly from beside them.

'No, he is not!' Kyle's voice rose angrily and his face turned red. 'He wouldn't ask your mum out. He doesn't even like your mum.'

'Yes, he does. He fancies her like mad—' Clara retorted swiftly, her cool manner slipping into something that was more like a teenage tantrum.

'Now, come along children. It's none of our business what your parents are talking about,' Zoë interjected soothingly as it seemed likely a war was about to erupt.

'All ready now?' Callum sauntered over to join them at that point.

'Yes, all ready,' Zoë tried to sound bright and cheerful.

Kyle glowered up at his father and Clara tossed her head and marched off to join her mother.

'What's the matter?' Callum said perplexed.

'Clara thinks that you fancy her mum like mad,' Alice said with the unreserved nonchalance only a five-year-old could get away with. 'But Zoë says you were just talking school business.'

'I see.' Callum looked over at Zoë before turning his attention back to his son. 'Well, it's not a subject for you youngsters to be discussing. Clara sounds as if she has watched too many episodes of *Neighbours*.'

'There, I told you that Dad wouldn't fancy Sally. She's not even nice,' Kyle hissed at his sister.

'That's enough, Kyle,' Callum said in a stern, faintly ominous tone. 'Sally is a lovely person and I won't have you talking like that.' He took the car keys from Zoë. 'Let's go, shall we?' he said heavily. 'Before the whole village joins in the conversation.'

Callum drove home. The journey was made in near silence. Kyle was sulking. Alice was asleep.

When they pulled into the yard, Callum had to lift Alice from the back seat, wrapping her gently within the folds of his coat to shelter her from the rain.

He took both children straight upstairs to bed, while Zoë put the kettle on.

He came back down a little while later. 'Alice wants to know if she can have a party for her birthday next week.'

'I thought she was asleep?'

'So did I. But she managed to open her eyes to put the request in.'

Zoë laughed. 'Well, I guess she's got to catch her dad while she can. What did you say?'

'I said I'd ask you.'

Zoë's eyebrows rose. 'You don't have to ask me.'

'I do. You'll be the one doing most of the hard work. She wants to invite her whole class.'

Zoë grinned. 'Well, that's no problem. I'll do it with pleasure.'

Callum's eyes moved over the softness of her complexion. 'Are you sure?'

'Course I'm sure.' She looked away from him suddenly

and, for no reason at all, she felt the tug of awareness between them. 'How old will Alice be?'

'Six. Thanks, Zoë.' She looked up at him and his gaze held hers. 'And thanks for covering for me tonight,' he said. 'I know you said you liked going to the theatre but I'm sure you didn't have our church hall in mind when you said it.'

'Well, it certainly makes a change from all those West End productions.' She tried to lighten the tension she felt by making the flip remark. Then she turned to make their coffee. She was so attracted to him: he only had to look at her like that and she felt herself go weak inside.

What was this chemistry that seemed to flare so swiftly, so suddenly, from nowhere? She didn't understand it at all.

'Kyle was great tonight, wasn't he?' She tried to turn her mind away from Callum, concentrate on the children. 'He recited that poem very proficiently.'

'Pity about his performance later,' Callum said gruffly.

'He's only little.' Zoë sipped her coffee and regarded him over the rim of the cup. 'Maybe you should sit down and talk to him about it.'

'And say what? Daddy has to have girlfriends?' Callum shook his head. 'He's filled with a lot of anger. I don't think it would help.'

Zoë had to fight the impulse to ask, 'Is Sally your girlfriend?' She was burning with curiosity to know the state of play between them, and that made her feel very uncomfortable because it was none of her business.

'It's as good a place as any to start,' she said gently, instead. 'I know you said your wife died a few years ago, but I do get the feeling he hasn't come to terms with it.'

'I know you do.' Callum frowned. 'But I honestly thought he had. He was so young when she died. He'd only just turned five. I didn't talk about it on any deep level.' He looked over at her then with a rueful grin. 'And, yes, I remember what you told me about it being good to talk about these things. But I thought we'd coped.'

'Maybe he was a bit young to understand when it happened, but you should try talking to him about it now,' Zoë suggested casually as she put her cup down. 'You don't know what goes through children's minds. He might be angry because his mother isn't here.'

Callum frowned. 'He wouldn't think that she wanted to leave him, would he?'

'He might.' Zoë shrugged. 'Maybe, when he sees you talking to another woman, he thinks he might lose you as well. You said yourself that he's frightened of change. You'll have to help him to realise that, no matter what, you're always there for him and that Daddy's friends are not a threat to his security. It's pretty scary being eight; you need to tell him these things.'

Callum finished his coffee and put his cup down on the table next to hers. His gaze moved searchingly over her face, noting the wide beauty of her eyes, the sincerity that shone from them, the soft curve of her lips. Her hair was woven back from her face in a severe plait showing the classical bone structure, the graceful long neck. A stray curl had dared to escape; it twirled in an unruly corkscrew fashion down the side of her neck.

Before he could think better of the action, he reached and brushed it back behind her ear. His fingers touched her skin in a feather-light caress that made a shiver run straight down her spine.

She moistened her lips nervously as she looked up into his eyes, shocked by the surge of desire that had sprung to life so easily. She wanted him to kiss her. She felt her heart thudding hard and painfully against her ribs. Feeling totally at a loss as to what to say or do, she did nothing, just looked up at him, waiting.

She had never met anyone with such incredibly dark

eyes; they seemed to look straight into her soul, and they seemed to speak to her in a basic, sensual way that made her hot all over.

He was the one to step back from the situation. He dropped his hand. 'I'll have a quiet word with him, see if I can fathom out where he's coming from,' he murmured.

'Yes.' She looked away, feeling embarrassed now. 'I think you should.' She picked up their cups from the table and put them in the sink. 'I'm going to turn in now, if you don't mind?'

'No, of course not. Don't forget, it's your day off tomorrow. Millie will be here to take the children to school.'

Suddenly they seemed to be talking in stilted phrases. Was it her imagination or had he been tempted to kiss her? If she had leaned closer…would he have met her halfway? Or was the attraction she felt just in her mind?

Her breath felt ragged and uncomfortable.

'Are you sleeping in my room or yours?' he asked quietly.

'Sorry?' She turned and looked at him then, her heart missing a beat.

'I just wondered if the joiner had arrived today. Is the window fixed?' He rephrased the question, a wry smile curving his lips.

'Oh.' Hell, now she felt even more awkward. She had thought, for one wild, irrational second, that he'd been inviting her to bed. And what would she have said if he was? Her eyes flicked involuntarily over the powerful physique. He had a wonderful body. He was too attractive by far. Even though he was her employer and she didn't know him that well, she might have been tempted against all common sense to say yes.

She shut that thought very firmly away.

'No…the joiner didn't come.'

'Typical.' Callum shrugged.

'So, I guess that means you're still in the spare room. Unless you want to swap?'

'No, I'll do the gentlemanly thing and let you have the draught-free room.'

'Thanks.' She grinned back at him. 'Well, goodnight, then.'

'Goodnight.' He watched her walk past the hall table. If he were a gentleman, he wouldn't have erased the message on the answering machine from her boyfriend, he thought with a sudden, severe pang of guilt.

He glanced at his watch. Maybe he should give Francis a ring now. Talk to him; tell him he was unhappy about the situation.

He walked out to the telephone and flicked through his phone book before dialling.

As he waited for Francis to answer his eye flicked over the lounge. Not only had Zoë placed flowers around it, she had moved some of the chairs to the other side of the room. It looked better, more homely somehow.

The phone was picked up. 'Hi, it's me,' he said in a very low tone. 'We've got to talk about this situation.'

Upstairs, Zoë finished brushing her teeth and left the bathroom door ajar as she went back to her bedroom. She heard the low murmur of Callum's voice. Something about the intimate timbre made her pause.

# CHAPTER SIX

ZoË walked briskly up over the bracken, the wind tingling against her face. The air was bracing and bitterly cold, the sky was a wild-peacock-blue, not a cloud to besmirch its brilliance.

As she got to the top of the hill, she contemplated the scene below. The mountains cradled the farmhouse; it was stark white against the green of the fields. Washing blew on the line. The trees in the orchard scattered blossom as the wind tugged at them mercilessly.

She sat down on a rock and studied the line of the land, noticing a small stream that wound down the mountain behind the house and then meandered through a field to the left of the farmyard.

In the far distance, to the right, she could see the cold wash of a lake. She wondered which lake it was. Windermere, perhaps.

Yes, this would be perfect, she thought as she took her sketch-book out of her bag. She'd do a few rough drawings here.

As she looked down at the house, she saw Millie coming out to take the washing off the line. Millie was a few years older than Zoë. She was a plump, very attractive girl with fresh clear skin and laughing hazel eyes. Zoë had liked her immediately. The two had shared a coffee before Zoë had left for a walk. She had learnt more about the village in those twenty minutes than she had in the few days she had been here.

She had heard all about Sally Fisher. She had left her husband some time ago, Millie had informed her. She had two children: one Kyle's age, one Alice's age. And she had serious designs on capturing Callum as husband number two.

Of course, she hadn't needed Millie to tell her that Sally was interested in Callum. That much was obvious. But, as for her wanting to marry him, that was pure speculation. Maybe she just wanted to have a fling with him. Maybe she'd been through a rough divorce and just wanted a bit of fun.

Zoë worked with quick, confident strokes building up the picture of the farm. Maybe Callum just wanted a bit of fun as well; he'd been through a rough time losing his wife. Millie had told her he had been absolutely devastated by her death. They'd been such a happy couple, so much in love.

It was at that point that Zoë had excused herself. Sitting at Callum's table discussing his late wife had suddenly felt like an extreme invasion of his privacy.

Millie seemed to think that, as yet, Callum hadn't taken Sally out. But Zoë had a feeling that that was about to change. She felt sure his phone call late last night had been to her. She hadn't been able to hear what he was saying, but it had sounded intimate, like a lover's call. Not that she'd tried to listen. She'd paused for one minute, that was all.

Then she'd lain in bed and thought about the way he had reached out and touched her in the kitchen. She must have imagined the desire in his eyes. The notion that he had been about to kiss her was probably a million miles away from the reality; more likely he had been thinking about Sally. He had simply been grateful to her for a bit of advice. Full stop. What an idiot she was.

'Hi, there.'

Zoë turned in surprise and saw Mark walking towards her.

'Thought it was you.' He grinned as he flopped down beside her. 'Heck, I'm out of condition.' He panted. 'The walk up here has almost finished me off.'

The wind ruffled his dark hair, giving him a boyishly attractive look. 'What are you doing?' He leaned over to look at her drawing. 'That's very good,' he murmured with genuine admiration.

'Thanks, it's just a hobby of mine.' She closed the sketch-book and put it back in her bag. 'Aren't you working today?'

'I'm on my way up to the house now to meet with Callum. One of his mares is in foal. I saw you from the road and thought I'd make a slight detour.'

She could see his car parked some distance away on the roadway. 'And you walked all the way up here, just to say hello. I am flattered.'

'Well, I suppose I did have an ulterior motive.' Mark grinned. 'I wanted to ask if you were free this Saturday night? There's a big bash on at Ashfield Hall. It used be called the Hunt Ball, but they don't have the hunt anymore, so it's just the Ball.'

'They call that progress.'

'Well, it is for the fox.' He grinned. 'So what do you say?'

She hesitated and he held up his hand. 'No strings and, despite what my brother told you, no funny business in my car.'

'How could I resist such an invitation?' She laughed.

'Thanks, Zoë, it should be a good night.'

'It does sound like fun,' she admitted.

He glanced at his watch. 'Better not keep Callum waiting. Do you want a lift back to the farm?'

'You're on.'

Callum arrived back at the house at the same time they did. They were laughing together as they got out of the car.

Mark was telling her an amusing story about a man who refused to pay his vet bills and how he got his money in the end. 'You are crazy, Mark,' she said, breathless from laughing.

'We've all known that for years,' Callum interjected, his gaze going from one to the other of them.

As always, the sight of Callum made her feel flustered. He had this way of meeting her eyes and making her feel as if he knew that she found him attractive.

'Where have you been, Mark, you're late?' he asked, looking back at his brother.

Mark paused in his tracks. 'Not too late?' he asked, horrified.

Callum shook his head and laughed. 'No. I reckon she'll be another few days at least. Come and take a look.'

The three of them walked around the side of the building. The stables were behind the barn. There were four horses in all. Three were grazing in the paddock; the one Mark had come to see was standing in one of the stalls.

'She looks rather dejected,' Zoë said with sympathy as she stroked a hand down over the mare's velvet brown coat.

'You would, too, if you had all the extra weight poor old Nell is carrying,' Callum answered, giving the mare a re-assuring pat on the neck as he went into the stall with Mark.

Mark examined the animal with a gentle thoroughness. 'Yes, I think you're right Callum,' he said at last. 'I don't think the foal is in a particular hurry to come. Maybe Sunday, or even the beginning of next week.'

Callum's attention wandered over towards Zoë who was standing framed in the doorway. She had left her hair loose today and the sun was glinting over it, turning it to the colour of ripened corn. She wore black bootleg trousers and a black polo-neck cashmere jumper that revealed a decidedly curvaceous body to its very best advantage.

She was stroking the horse, her concentration solely on the animal, her manner gentle and soothing.

'We'll wait until Monday. See what happens. If she hasn't started naturally by then, I'll see about giving her a helping hand. What do you think?' Mark looked up when there was no immediate reply. He saw his brother's gaze resting on Zoë, saw an expression in his eye that he hadn't seen there for a long time. 'Callum?'

'Sorry?' Callum turned. 'Yes, Monday is fine. As long as leaving her doesn't pose a risk?'

'No, she's fine for now. We'll just have to keep an eye on her.'

They left the stable and Mark paused to wash his hands at an outside tap. 'Sally was asking me if you are going to the party at Ashfield Hall on Saturday,' he told Callum nonchalantly.

'I don't know yet. Depends if I can get Tom to cover for me here.'

Mark straightened and met his brother's eye. 'If you are, maybe we could make up a foursome?'

'Who would the foursome be?' Callum asked.

'You, Sally, me and Zoë.'

'I see.' Callum glanced over at Zoë and, for some reason, the dark steady gaze made her feel as if she had done something she shouldn't.

He shrugged. 'I'll ring Sally and ask her. Only, I'll have to check first with Ellen to see if she'll babysit.'

'Oh!' Zoë shook her head. 'I'm sorry Callum, did you want me to babysit for you? I will if you want.'

'No, you won't,' Mark interrupted briskly. 'You can't babysit. You're coming to the party with me—'

'It's OK,' Callum cut across them swiftly. 'I said I'd ask Ellen.'

'Fine.' Mark smiled over at Zoë. 'Right, if I don't see you before, I'll see you Saturday night.'

She nodded and was completely taken aback when he reached and gave her a quick kiss on the cheek.

'I'll pick you up about eight.'

She wondered suddenly if she had made a mistake accepting the invitation. She liked Mark, but she didn't want him to get the wrong idea. She wasn't romantically interested in him and had only agreed to go out because it sounded like fun, that was all.

As the two men walked away towards Mark's car, Zoë wandered down to the paddock to have a closer look at the horses.

Callum joined her a little while later. He leaned on the fence beside her. 'Do you ride?' he asked.

'Yes, I do.'

'I'm going to ride up to one of the fields at the far side of the property, if you'd like to come with me? There's a wall up there that I need to repair.'

She smiled at him. 'I'd really like that, thanks.'

He nodded. 'Which horse do you want? Mine is—'

'The grey stallion,' she guessed. 'He's highly strung, powerful and very much a man's horse. Am I right?'

'OK, clever clogs.' He grinned.

'I'll take the bay,' she said, her gaze moving to the magnificent animal at the far side. Her coat a gleaming, polished red-brown, her dark mane and tail flowing like silk as she pranced like a ballerina around the others.

For a moment, Callum hesitated. Then he opened the gate. 'I'll saddle her up for you.'

It had been a long time since Zoë had ridden; she had forgotten how much she loved it. How exhilarating it was to feel the air rushing against her skin, the thump of her heart as her body and the horse, merged and blended into one fluid movement across the open countryside.

They had started out at a sedate pace and then, as Zoë's horse had tugged impatiently at the reins, she had allowed it its head and they were racing now over the landscape, Callum slightly ahead of her. He was a skilled horseman, controlling the powerful animal with ease.

'That was fabulous,' she said breathlessly as Callum reigned in his horse.

'It blew away a few cobwebs,' he agreed. 'We'll have to walk for a while from here.' He nodded towards a rocky track that wound precariously around the side of a deep gorge.

'Is this all your land?' Zoë asked him as they both dismounted to walk side by side along the path, leading their horses.

'Yes, up to the very far ridge.' He nodded to a distant range of foothills that glowed purple against the blue of the sky. There was a swathe of forest beneath it, the trees starting to unfurl their green springtime colours after the starkness of winter.

'It's beautiful,' she murmured. 'So peaceful.'

'Yes, I must admit I do love it here.'

'You don't miss Cheshire, then?'

He shook his head. 'Cheshire is a beautiful county, but it's much more manicured. I like the rugged, untamed features of Cumbria.'

'Did you own a farm in Cheshire?' Zoë asked him curiously.

'No.' He laughed and slanted her a wry look. 'I was a stockbroker. Spent all my days going into Manchester and looking at share prices.'

Zoë was surprised. 'So what made you decide to become a farmer?'

'I didn't really decide to become a farmer.' He shook his head. 'I fell in love with a farmer's daughter and it rather happened overnight. One day I was dressed in a suit, carrying a briefcase, the next I was wading in here, wearing gumboots, helping Helen's father.'

'So this was Helen's family farm?'

'Yes. She ran a riding stables here, which was how we met. I was up for a short break visiting Mark, and I came to hire a horse.'

'Funny old thing, fate, isn't it?' Zoë said lightly. 'Makes you wonder if life is mapped out for you and you're just a pawn in the grand scheme of things.'

'Maybe.' Callum grinned. 'I certainly never envisaged myself running a farm. Mark was always the one into the great outdoors. I was the office type, into computers and the *Financial Times*.'

'Do you ever miss wearing the suit and carrying the briefcase?'

'No. Never. I still dabble a bit with stocks and shares though. Some habits die hard.' He grinned. 'And it's probably just as well that they do. It's kept the farm ticking over nicely through some tough times. That, and—' He stopped himself suddenly. He'd been going to say, 'That, and having a friend in high places,' but he couldn't impart that piece of information. She might ask who the friend was, and he could hardly inform her it was her father.

'That, and…?' she prompted him.

He wavered for just a second on the verge of telling her he knew Francis; he wanted to clear the air. He wanted to ask her outright about Mr Unsuitable.

Francis had told him on the phone last night that he'd been around to see her boyfriend and he now thought it wasn't going to be as easy to get rid of him as he had first thought.

'You'll have to try and keep her there a bit longer,' Francis had pleaded. 'And, under no circumstances, allow her to talk to him on the phone.'

'That's ridiculous,' Callum had argued. 'How am I going to stop her? And I doubt she will stay on longer. She's already told me she must return back to London for the second week of April.'

'Why the second week in April?' Francis had immediately been suspicious. 'You don't think she's set a wedding date, do you?'

The conversation and the question had plagued Callum all night. He remembered Matthew's voice on the answering machine. 'Everything is set for the fifteenth.' Was that a wedding date? Maybe he should try to find out.

He looked over at her, realising that she was waiting for him to continue. He wouldn't mention Francis; he'd have to tread carefully. What had they been talking about? Oh, yes, the farm. 'That, and a lot of hard work,' he said instead.

She stumbled on the uneven ground and he reached out a hand to steady her. 'Are you OK?' His hand rested for a minute longer than was strictly necessary around her waist.

'Yes. Sorry, I should watch where I'm going.' There was a rush of adrenalin at the contact and the feeling that she would have welcomed him coming even closer. What was the matter with her? she wondered with trepidation. She had never known a man to have this effect on her before. It was as if her every nerve ending was supersensitive where he was concerned.

They reached a clearing and, ahead of them on the smooth grassy bank, was the damaged wall that Callum had set out to repair.

Zoë sat down on a rock and watched him as he worked. 'Quite an art to that,' she remarked after a few minutes.

'Drystone walling is a skill that's been handed down through the generations around here. It's quite a distinctive characteristic of the landscape. Do you want to have a go at it?'

'I'll try.' She moved to kneel beside him as he showed her what to do.

'No, not like that.' He caught hold of her hands. They were smooth and soft in his. 'Place them like this.' He turned them so that the rock slid neatly to rest. 'See, very effective, isn't it?'

The only effect Zoë could think of was the one he was having on her. She felt her heart drumming against her chest, she felt peculiarly light-headed.

'I think I've got the hang of it now,' she muttered, pulling her hand away from his. He watched as she built up a few pieces of the wall.

'Yes, not bad, you're a fast learner.' He grinned.

'So, if I ever get fed up with life in London, you'd give me a job as a labourer?' she asked with a smile.

'I'd consider you for the position,' he agreed, a teasing glint in his eye. 'But, of course, you'd have to prove yourself a bit more first.'

'In what way?' She sat back on her heels, her hands on her hips.

'In every way. I wouldn't go easy on you just because you're a woman, you know. I believe equal rights works both ways. You'd have to pull your weight with the men.'

'No problem,' she said confidently.

It probably wouldn't be for her, he decided as he continued to work alongside her. She was a mere slip of a thing, very slender, very feminine. Yet, she gave the impression of determination, as if she could do anything if she really wanted to.

'But it's not help out on the farm that I need. It's help in the house.' He looked across at her then. 'But, of course, you wouldn't want to leave London, would you?'

'Depends on the inducement,' she answered quietly. She finished the area she was working on and sat back, dusting her hands on the grass.

'What about your boyfriend? I kind of got the impression it was a serious relationship.'

KATHRYN ROSS                    93

'What gives you that idea?'

'You've been on the phone to him nearly every night.'

'Have I?' She grinned. 'If I recall rightly, you were the one using the phone late last night.'

He almost dropped the last stone. Had she heard him talking to her father?

She noticed the flicker of unease in his eyes as he looked at her. So it was all right for him to talk about her relationships but not the other way around, she thought with annoyance. Well, she wasn't playing at that. 'Now, that's what I call serious. You'd only just said goodnight to Sally a couple of hours earlier.'

'What makes you think I was talking to Sally?' He tried to keep the relief from his voice. For a second he had thought she knew. He was surprised by how much that panicked him. Hadn't he been deliberating telling her the truth a little while ago, anyway?

'I'm right though, aren't I?' she said with unwavering conviction.

She seemed so certain that Callum found himself shrugging. 'You shouldn't be listening in to my phone calls.' That was rich, he thought dryly, considering he'd been listening to all of hers.

'I was not listening,' she said outraged.

Obviously not, he thought. How had he got himself involved in Francis's family problems, he wondered as the now familiar curl of guilt stirred to life inside him.

But he was involved, so he should go ahead, try and find out the state of play between her and this guy. 'Anyway,' he murmured. 'Getting back to our original conversation. I don't expect your boyfriend would let you move up here, even if I was offering a more permanent job.'

Zoë's eyebrows rose. 'He's a boyfriend not a warden,' she said flippantly.

'If he's serious about you, he won't be very happy to

learn that you are going out with Mark on Saturday,' he remarked casually after a moment.

'I don't think he'll mind.' Zoë shrugged. 'It's just a bit of fun, after all. And Mark has assured me his intentions are honourable.'

They'd have to be, Callum thought decisively, because he didn't intend leaving his brother alone with Zoë. In fact, he intended to take him up on that offer of a foursome. That was if Sally was disposed towards a double date of course. He'd ring her tonight.

Francis hadn't sent his daughter up here for her to land in the clutches of another charmer. As much as he loved his brother, he was well aware that, where women were concerned, he was a bit of a philanderer.

'So your boyfriend back in London isn't the jealous type, I take it.' He made one last attempt at trying to draw her out on the subject.

'No, not really, our relationship isn't like that. Matt's really sweet, very easy going.'

Sweet. Callum's lips twisted in a derisory smile. 'If you don't mind me saying, it doesn't sound very much like a grand passion.'

Zoë had been in the process of relaxing back against the wall, her face turned up towards the sun, her eyes closed. They opened wide now to glance sharply over at Callum.

'Sorry.' He held up his hands. 'But, when someone is passionately in love, they're not usually sweet and easy going when the love of their life goes out on a date with someone else.'

'With respect, Callum, you don't know anything about my relationship with Matt. So I'd rather you didn't comment,' she retorted sharply. 'I wouldn't dream of speculating about your relationship with Sally Fisher.'

'You just did a few minutes ago.'

'No, I didn't. I said you'd phoned her, that's all.'

'Well, anyway, there's nothing to speculate about.'

'Isn't there?'

'No. I'm taking her out on a first date. It's not even an affair, yet.'

Callum frowned and wondered how she had managed to change the subject towards him. Plus she'd got more information out of him than he had out of her, without even trying very hard. He frowned.

Not an affair…*yet*. That one word echoed in Zoë's mind for a moment. It seemed obvious that it would be soon. But it had nothing to do with her; she didn't even know why she was thinking about it.

'Speaking of Saturday.' She changed the subject swiftly. 'Do you think you should ask Ellen to babysit?'

'Why not?'

Zoë hesitated, mindful of the fact that she had told Callum's mother she wouldn't divulge she wasn't well. 'I just thought she looked a little tired last time I saw her.'

'When did you see her?'

'Oh, I forgot to tell you, she called the other night to see the children.'

'Was she helping with the housework?'

'No, she was not!' Zoë glared at him. 'Sometimes I get the feeling you don't have much faith in my abilities.'

'Oh, it's not that Zoë. It's just Mum does tend to take over a lot when it comes to the housework. I tell her not to do so much, but she doesn't listen. Even when Millie is there she sometimes comes fussing around.'

'Well, she didn't do any housework while I was there.' She held his eyes steadily. 'And let me tell you, I'm more than capable of running your house and looking after your children, and I could probably run the farm in my spare time as well if I had a mind to.'

He smiled. She most likely damn well could, he found

himself thinking dryly. He had certainly revised his earlier opinions about her. 'I never intended to suggest otherwise.'

She gave him a wry look, a look that made him feel a bit uncomfortable. OK, maybe he had underestimated her at first, judged her harshly. But, then, Francis had influenced those preconceptions.

He looked away from her. 'Well, as I'm all finished here, I suppose we should go.'

'Yes. I suppose so.' She got to her feet, ignoring the hand he held out to her, pretending to sweep the grass off her trousers as if she hadn't seen it.

'Are we going back the way we came?' Zoë pulled her horse around and patted its flank soothingly.

'Maybe we should.' Callum pointed to a gate further over. 'We could go that way. It's a straight route downhill. Only problem is you've got to cross the stream and there are a few jumps to negotiate.'

'You don't think I'm up to it?' She fixed him with that steady gaze he was starting to get used to.

'I didn't say that.'

'Good.' Effortlessly Zoë pulled herself up into the saddle. 'Because I could ride you under the table.'

He grinned. 'Sounds interesting.'

She felt heat whipping into her face as she looked at the dark humour in his eyes. 'Tell you what, I'll race you back,' she challenged, her eyes dancing with mischief.

He smiled. 'You can try. But I'll win.'

'How much do you want to bet?' She'd teach him, she thought with a tinge of annoyance.

He thought about it for a moment, and then turned his horse around so that he could mount. 'Loser buys a bottle of champagne at the party on Saturday.'

'You're on. First back at the stables wins.'

He hadn't even settled himself in the saddle and she had taken off. She cleared the low part of the wall and was halfway down the next field before he had even started his pursuit.

He smiled as he watched her, a flicker of admiration in his eye as he noticed how expertly she handled the highly-bred horse, her blonde hair streaming out behind her, her slender body raised from the saddle leaning forward urging the animal forward.

Zoë didn't dare look around to see where Callum was until she had the farm in sight. Only then was she confident enough to turn in the saddle and search for him. He was nowhere to be seen.

She was smiling to herself and feeling smugly pleased as she trotted into the courtyard behind the house. The feeling was short-lived, however, as she saw Callum standing by the stables, nonchalantly waiting for her.

'How did you do that?' she asked perplexed. 'I was well-ahead of you and I didn't see you pass me.'

'Rule number one: don't issue challenges when you don't know the lie of the land.' He caught hold of her horse as she stopped beside him and reached to help her dismount. 'You owe me a bottle of champagne, I believe.'

'And I believe you must have cheated.' Her feet touched the ground and she turned, only to find herself sandwiched between him and the horse.

'That's a very serious accusation,' he murmured, a glint of humour in his dark eyes. 'I hope you are going to take it back.'

'No, I am not.' She met his gaze with determination, trying to ignore the thump of her heart. 'Admit it, you must have taken a short cut.'

'The challenge was: first back here,' he said with a grin. 'You didn't stipulate how we got back.'

'I didn't think I had to. It was supposed to be a race.' Her eyes sparkled with defiance. 'So I think you should buy the bottle of champagne because you cheated.'

'That word isn't in my vocabulary.' He shook his head, a mock-serious light in his dark eyes. 'I think you had better take back the accusation or you might be sorry.'

'And if I don't, what are you going to do?' She put a hand on her hip, a smile curving the soft contours of her lips.

He smiled back at her. The playful challenge amused him. 'I don't know.' He pretended to think about it for a moment. 'I could banish you to the cold spare bedroom where I freeze every night.'

'Do you?' She was momentarily distracted from their banter.

He grinned. Then his eyes moved over her lips. 'Or I could take a more interesting revenge.' His voice lowered to a husky sound that was very seductive. She found herself moistening her lips; she felt her body responding very positively to him. She wanted him to kiss her.

The horse moved behind her and she felt herself pressed closer against his body. She tilted her head and met his eye.

He could see the challenge in the beauty of her eyes. She was daring him to kiss her, he felt it very strongly. He also felt desire very strongly. He told himself that he should move back from her; there were a million sensible reasons why kissing her was a bad idea. And at the head of that list was the fact that he hadn't been honest with her. He was in league with her father. That knowledge should have made him hesitate, move away from her. But she was so close and so beautiful. He couldn't resist.

He lowered his head and his lips met hers in a sizzling, passionate kiss. He told himself that he was only going to let it continue for a moment, just a brief, teasing intimacy that he would laugh off.

Trouble was, that once he tasted her, he couldn't stop. Her lips were provocatively soft, inviting. She wound her arms up and rested her hands on his shoulder, responding hungrily to him.

When they finally broke apart, they were both breathing heavily and they could only stare at each other in a kind of dazed shock.

'Wow!' He was the first to speak, his lips curving into a somewhat bemused smile.

'I shouldn't have done that, should I?' he asked wryly.

'I suppose not.' Her voice wasn't at all steady.

'Sorry.' He stepped back feeling suddenly mortified. 'Look, it was all my fault.'

Zoë wasn't so sure she agreed with that. She had wanted him to touch her; her body had been on fire with a desire that was very illogical. How could she feel this much need for a man she barely knew, moreover a man who was interested in another woman?

'Shall we just put it down to a moment of madness and forget it?' His voice held a brusque edge. Maybe he, too, was thinking about Sally.

'Might be best.' Her eyes moved over the handsome contours of his face. Trouble was, she didn't know if she could forget it.

# CHAPTER SEVEN

'YOU look very pretty,' Alice told her solemnly from the doorway.

'Thank you, Alice.' Zoë turned from the dressing table to look at the little girl.

'You'll be the prettiest girl at the party,' Alice said with conviction. 'Will Daddy dance with you?'

'I don't know.' Zoë laughed.

Behind the light-hearted conversation, she felt a twinge of nervous anticipation. It was two days now since Callum had kissed her. She had tried to pretend it hadn't happened, but there had been an atmosphere between them ever since.

When he was at home, she tried to keep out of his way. She'd done everything she could to avoid having to even glance at him directly. They were practically tiptoeing around each other, making polite comments about the weather but, under all of that, Zoë felt as if there was a time bomb ticking as if there was unfinished business between them, and the tension was killing her.

The last thing she needed was this party tonight. The thought of being with Callum in a foursome all evening was enough to push her temperature up through the ceiling.

'Uncle Mark is here,' Alice said.

'Oh, good.' Zoë tried to sound enthusiastic. 'Tell him I'll be down in a minute.'

As Alice raced eagerly to do as she was asked, Zoë gave her reflection a last critical glance. She hadn't brought anything particularly dressy with her so, on Millie's recommendation, she'd gone to a small boutique in Kendal late on Thursday afternoon to buy something.

The result was a powder-blue dress in a softly shimmering material. It had minimal shoestring straps that showed the perfect creamy sweep of her neck and shoulders and, to complement this, she had swept her hair up on top of her head in a sophisticated style.

The only thing she had reservations about was the fact that the long skirt had a deep split up one side that, as she sat down, showed a very provocative glimpse of her legs.

She'd just have to pull the material across when she took a seat. Hopefully she'd stand all evening, she thought with a wry grin. She picked up her wrap and left the room.

As she walked down the corridor, she hesitated outside Kyle's doorway. His father had sent him to his room earlier after a particularly bad tantrum at the dinner table.

On impulse, she knocked on the bedroom door and put her head around. Kyle was sitting on his bed, looking down at the pages of his *Dandy* annual with a fierce frown of concentration.

'Everything all right, Kyle?' she asked softly.

He didn't answer.

Zoë walked further into the room and sat down next to him on the bed.

'Tell you what, why don't you go downstairs and say you're sorry to Daddy. Then everything will be OK.'

'No.'

'What's the matter Kyle?' Zoë asked softly. She reached out to touch his arm. 'Why don't you tell me what's really bothering you, hmm?'

The child hesitated for a moment. 'Clara told me at school yesterday that Dad is taking her mum out tonight.'

'I see.' Zoë hesitated. 'It's just a party, Kyle. Lots of people will be there. You don't want your daddy to be unhappy, do you?'

Kyle shook his head.

'Or lonely?'

Again, Kyle shook his head. 'I just don't want him to go out with Clara's mum,' he said glumly. 'I don't like Clara.'

Zoë suppressed a smile. Strangely enough, she felt the same way about Sally Fisher, and for no real good reason.

'Come on downstairs and say goodnight to Daddy.' She held out her hand and, tentatively, Kyle put down his annual and took it.

Together they went down the stairs.

Callum was standing with his back to the mantelpiece in the lounge, talking to Mark. Both men looked over at her as she walked in. Both looked extremely handsome in dark suits. But it was Callum who held her attention. He looked incredible. She had never seen him in anything other than casual attire before. He looked good in jeans, but the suit emphasised just how handsome he was. The width of his shoulders, the powerful well-honed body was shown to its best advantage. The result was Zoë's stomach started to tie up into little knots of something that felt very much like longing.

'Daddy, I'm sorry.' Kyle flung himself across the room towards his father, and Callum swept him up to give him a hug.

'It's OK,' he said gently, giving the child a kiss and holding him tight.

Across the room, he met Zoë's eyes for the first time since their kiss. She felt her heart somersault from her chest into her stomach and back again.

'You look fantastic, Zoë,' Mark said, making her wrench her eyes away from Callum.

'Thanks.' She smiled at him. 'Hope I haven't kept you waiting too long.'

'Not at all.' Mark glanced at his watch. 'But, as Sally is expecting to be picked up at eight-thirty, we should leave now.'

'Better not keep that one waiting,' Millie said as she came through from the kitchen with a bowl of popcorn for the children. She grinned mischievously over at Callum. 'She'll be counting the seconds.'

'I doubt it.' Callum took the teasing with an easy smile. 'But it never does to keep a lady waiting.' He ruffled Kyle's hair. 'You kids be good for Millie, bed at the usual time.'

'Are you going to dance with Zoë, Daddy?' Alice asked. 'I think you should.'

'Hey!' Mark cut in with a grin. 'Uncle Mark is dancing with Zoë tonight.'

Callum bent down and gave his daughter a kiss. 'I'll ask her later,' he said in a mock whisper.

Zoë tried not to feel embarrassed. They were just joking. But, even so, she couldn't bring herself to look over at Callum. She busied herself instead with wrapping herself up and reaching for her handbag.

It was cold outside. The frost glittered hard on the roof of Mark's car and on the windscreen. 'You wouldn't believe I'd only just got here, would you?' he complained as he unlocked the vehicle and set about scraping the ice away.

Zoë slipped into the small back seat and Callum got into the passenger seat at the front.

'It's at times like this that the fireside and the TV seem inviting,' Zoë remarked, shivering.

Callum turned to look at her. 'Would you like me to go back into the house and get you a travel rug?'

She shook her head. 'No. I'll be fine once the heater has got warmed up.'

He didn't turn back, but continued to watch her. It was slightly unnerving because she couldn't see the expression on his face in the darkness of the car but, by contrast, the light coming from the house lit up her face.

'Thanks for having a talk with Kyle tonight,' he said. 'I

tried earlier, but he wouldn't tell me what was bothering him. Whatever you said, it worked wonders.'

'At least he seemed happier.'

'Yes.' There was silence between them for a moment. She looked very pale in the glow of light from the house. Her eyes, incredibly green, looked almost too large for her face.

'Did he tell you what was troubling him?'

'Clara informed him that you were taking Sally out and he wasn't happy about it.' She looked away from him wondering if maybe she shouldn't have said that. 'But I think it's because he doesn't like Clara.'

'Perhaps.'

Mark climbed into the car. 'Hell, I'm freezing now,' he complained.

They set off at a slow pace down the winding drive towards the road. It was a clear night, the moon hung low in the sky silhouetting the top of the mountains with silvery light and reflecting in the deep waters of the lake.

Zoë found herself wishing that she were alone with Callum, then hated herself for the thought. He was dating someone else, she told herself fiercely. She must stop this.

It didn't seem to take long to reach the cottage where Sally lived. It was a picturesque building at the edge of the village. She was waiting for them, looking out from a downstairs window. She gave them a wave as Mark pulled the car up and the next moment she was outside.

Callum got out to open the back passenger door for her. 'Hello, darling.' She stood on tiptoe and kissed him on the cheek.

Zoë experienced a definite thrust of jealousy. She looked away, willing herself not to be like this. She was only here for another week. She couldn't get embroiled in Callum's love life.

'Hi, Mark.' She slid in beside Zoë. Her perfume was

overpowering. It made Zoë want to sneeze. 'How are things?'

'Not so bad, looking up all the time.' Mark grinned.

Sally looked over at Zoë. 'I didn't expect you to be here,' she said with a very cool smile. 'Who's babysitting for you tonight, Callum?'

'Millie.'

'That's a point,' Mark said. 'Why didn't you ask Mum?'

'Zoë mentioned that Mum might still be feeling a bit tired, so I asked Millie instead.'

'What nonsense,' Sally cut across Callum swiftly. 'I saw Ellen in the village only a few days ago and she was looking radiantly fit.'

'I don't know, Sally. I called in on her this morning and I didn't think she looked well,' Callum murmured. 'I'm actually quite worried about her.'

'I'll call by tomorrow and check on her,' Mark said. He pulled the car through an imposing set of high gates.

Up ahead a Georgian mansion was ablaze with light. It was a spectacular house, very regal, very much the type of dwelling Zoë could imagine the hunt gathering at.

Mark parked the car and they joined the crowds of people going up the front steps.

A member of staff took their wraps and they made their way through the vast entrance hall to the splendour of the ballroom.

Zoë noticed that Sally had linked her arm with Callum. She looked very attractive in a long black velvet dress with a plunging neckline. She was smiling up at him, talking animatedly.

'They seem to be getting along quite well, don't they?' Mark commented, following her gaze.

'Yes, they do.' Zoë smiled and looked away.

'Just goes to show that perseverance pays off eventually.'

Mark grimaced. 'Sally has chased Callum relentlessly these last few months. Asked him out, hounded him in fact.'

Zoë's eyebrows rose. 'Did Callum tell you that?'

'Hell, no. Cal is far too much of a gentleman to say something like that.' Mark laughed. 'No, it's just been blatantly obvious that she has her sights set on him. Has done ever since her affair fizzled out with local GP, Ted Forrester.'

A band struck up at the end of the room and the noise was so deafening that Zoë had to lean closer to him to hear.

'He's here tonight.' Mark nodded his head over towards a distinguished-looking man, tall with greying hair. 'Sally left her husband for Forrester.'

'How long ago is it since she split up with Forrester?'

'I don't know, a couple of months maybe, at most.'

'It's not very long. She could still be on the rebound.'

'Perhaps.' Mark shrugged. 'I don't care as long as Callum has a good time. He's buried himself alive in that farm and the children for too long since Helen died.'

'Well, he has to put his children first. They have been upset and depressed as well.'

Mark nodded. His eyes moved over her face for a moment as if noting everything about her. 'You really like the kids, don't you?'

'Yes, they are lovely children.'

'And Callum?'

Zoë hoped she wasn't blushing. 'He…he's OK.'

Mark nodded and smiled.

Callum came over to join them. He was carrying a bottle of champagne and four glasses. 'There's a table over here,' he said. 'Shall we sit down?'

They followed him to where Sally was waiting. Zoë couldn't help but notice that she didn't look very pleased at the fact that they were joining her.

'Champagne?' Mark said as he noticed the bottle Callum held. 'I'm impressed.'

Zoë's eyes brushed with Callum's.

'Some things are worth splashing out on,' he said with a wry grin. He popped the cork and filled the glasses, handing the first one over to Zoë. 'Anyway, it's all in a good cause tonight.'

Her hand touched against his as she took the glass; she felt the tingle all the way down to her toes.

The band played a well-known love song. 'I adore this song,' Sally gushed. 'Come and dance with me, Callum.'

Zoë watched as he led her on to the dance floor. She hastily averted her gaze as Sally moved into his arms her head resting against his chest.

'So.' She had to work very hard trying to sound bright and cheerful because, suddenly, it was a million miles away from how she was feeling. 'What did Callum mean when he said it's in a good cause tonight?'

'All the profits from the ball are going to the RSPCA.'

'Oh. I see.'

'Do you want to dance?' Mark asked.

She glanced back at the dance floor. It was packed with people and she couldn't see Sally now, just the top of Callum's head over the crowd.

'OK.' She smiled at Mark.

'Let me just warn you,' he said as he took hold of her hand, 'I have two left feet.'

'Now you tell me.'

'So how much longer will you be working for Callum?' Mark asked conversationally as they squeezed onto the edge of the floor and he took her into his arms.

'About another week or so.'

'Can't you stay any longer?'

'Maybe a few days, but not much more,' Zoë answered, thinking about her art exhibition. She had to be back in

London for that. The thought of the exhibition made butterflies stir inside. She had worked so hard on her paintings; just say they weren't well received, and just say none of them sold? Of course, they would sell, she told herself fiercely. She had to be confident. She would also have to be back in London well in time to check everything was organised. She couldn't leave it all to Matt.

'Shame,' Mark murmured.

He turned her and she could see Callum again. He was saying something to Sally, his head bent, his lips close to her ear.

Zoë turned her attention firmly back to Mark.

'I suppose you'll be looking forward to getting back to the big city.'

'In some ways.' She shrugged. 'I like popping into the big stores every now and then but, apart from that, it's a relief to be out of the traffic fumes and the hectic pace. I think maybe I'm a bit of a country girl at heart.'

Mark grinned. 'A bit like Callum. I never thought he was the country-loving type at all. He's really surprised me.'

'He was telling me how he came up here for a short break and ended up staying.'

'Ended up bailing the farm out of a financial mess,' Mark said dryly. 'Helen's father had been trying to sell it for ages but didn't have any offers, and it was heading slowly towards bankruptcy. Then in rode Callum on his white charger and his city head for figures and turned it around.'

'He must have been very much in love with Helen.'

'Yes. They made a great couple.' Mark shook his head sadly. 'Sometimes I think he should sell up and make a fresh start somewhere else; there are too many memories at that farm for him.'

'But they are happy memories.'

'Doesn't make them any less painful.' Mark met her eyes. 'But Cal won't hear of leaving. Plus the farm is doing

OK, which, given the current economic climate for farming, is pretty miraculous.'

'Due, in no small part, to Callum's financial brain, I suppose.' Zoë grinned.

'And a lucrative contract from a certain major supermarket chain. Callum has friends in high places.'

'I suppose every little helps.' Zoë was distracted, looking around for Callum now. She couldn't see him.

The music changed to a more energetic disco beat. 'I think that's my cue to sit down.' Mark laughed.

When they returned to the table Callum was already there and on his own.

Mark pulled out Zoë's chair for her, but he didn't sit down himself, 'I'm just going to get a soft drink at the bar. Do you want anything?'

Zoë shook her head.

Callum reached across and topped up her glass with champagne. 'We'll stick to this as we're not driving,' he said easily.

As Mark left them alone there was an awkward silence for a moment, filled with the thump of a disco beat that seemed to match Zoë's heart rate.

'Thanks for the champagne.' She looked over at him and smiled.

'Never let it be said that I reneged on a bet,' he said with a grin.

'So, you admit that you were cheating?'

'No, I do not.' There was a spark of devilment in his dark eyes as he looked at her. 'Do you admit to being provocative?'

'I don't know what you mean.' She looked at him with wide-eyed innocence and hoped that she wasn't blushing.'

He smiled. 'You look extremely beautiful tonight, by the way.'

The compliment was murmured in a very low, husky

tone but she heard it clearly over the music and it made her body go hot inside.

'It's probably politically incorrect to tell an employee that she's beautiful,' she said light-heartedly.

He laughed. 'Well, I like to fly in the face of convention.'

'You are definitely doing that,' she agreed. 'Where is your date?'

He shook his head. 'I don't know. Maybe she's dumped me.'

'I doubt it.' Zoë tore her eyes away from him and searched the crowds, but there was no sign of Sally, or Mark for that matter.

'How about a dance?' Callum asked suddenly. 'I did promise Alice I'd ask.'

Zoë hesitated. She very much wanted to dance with him, only the thought of getting too close scared her. The memory of the way he had kissed her the other day was still so real, so disturbingly sensual. She was worried that if he touched her, if he held her, she might want to repeat the sensation all over again, right here, right now.

'What's the matter, not feeling energetic?' He grinned. 'Aren't you the woman who told me you could run my house, look after my children and probably manage the farm in her spare time? Don't tell me you'd have no energy left over for disco dancing?'

She grinned back at him. 'I could dance you under the table, Callum.'

'Now, that sounds interesting.' He held out his hand to her as she pushed her chair back. 'First one who needs to sit down buys the next bottle of champagne?'

'I'm not falling for that.' She laughed. 'You'll only cheat.' She slipped her hand into his and allowed him to lead the way through the crowds to the centre of the floor.

He was a good dancer, she thought as they moved together to the gyrating rhythm. She moved closer, her body swaying with sinuous, graceful movements.

He watched the way she moved, the willowy sway of her body, the lissom movements somehow sensually inviting, provocatively intimate, yet she seemed unaware of him, lost in the music.

The coloured lights from the stage played over her, washing her in blue then gold. Then, as the beat of the music slowed, he reached out and took her into his arms.

The possessive touch of his hand on her waist felt as if it was burning through her dress. She tried very hard to ignore the sensual thrill, but it was nigh on impossible when her body was in chaos and her heart was in overdrive.

'That's better.' He murmured the words against her ear, causing ripples of tingling pleasure to flow through her.

'Don't tell me you're tired?' From somewhere she managed to summon the flippant remark.

'Not at all.' His hand rested lightly on the small of her back, but it felt like a band of possession. 'I could dance the night away.'

So could I, Zoë thought dreamily as she allowed herself the pleasure of relaxing against him. She breathed in the fresh scent of his cologne, her head resting against the breadth of his chest. Suddenly she wondered what it would be like to make love with him, to lie naked against that physically powerful body as he possessed her totally.

The thought sent alarm bells ringing furiously inside her. 'I think we should sit down,' she said abruptly pulling away from him. 'Sally and Mark will be wondering where we are.'

He didn't argue. Instead, he placed a guiding hand at her back as they returned to their table.

Sally and Mark were deep in conversation, their heads close. 'There you are.' Sally looked up, her eyes overbright as they moved from Callum to Zoë.

'Zoë was showing me just how energetic she is.' Callum grinned. He reached for the bottle of champagne and topped up their glasses.

Across the table, Zoë met Sally's brooding, very unfriendly stare.

'Well, it's fun to get into the party spirit,' Zoë said brightly, then cringed inside at how inane that sounded. Sally was obviously furious that she had danced with Callum.

'I believe you are organising a party for Alice's birthday.' Sally turned her attention to Callum, pointedly ignoring Zoë.

'Yes, on Monday, after school. You'll have to bring the girls.'

'I'll look forward to it.' Sally's lips curved into a pleased smile, her good humour instantly restored. 'I'll give a helping hand with the organisation if you'd like?'

'Well, that's Zoë's domain.' Callum looked across at her. 'Do you need any help, Zoë?'

'I think I've got everything pretty much covered, thanks,' Zoë smiled politely at the other woman.

'You and I can relax over a bottle of wine, then, Callum, while the kiddies enjoy themselves.'

Zoë reached for her glass of champagne. The prospect of Sally hanging around at Monday's party was not a welcome one.

Sally completely monopolised Callum's attention after that, talking about people in the village that Zoë didn't know, sitting with her shoulder turned so that Zoë was, effectively, blocked out. Not that she was bothered, Mark was good company and they kept up a light-hearted repartee until the buffet was served in the adjoining room.

From time to time, though, she would catch Callum's gaze and then it would feel as if everything else faded to oblivion, as if it was just the two of them, alone. It was the strangest sensation, one that made her shiver with an anticipation of something she couldn't begin to understand.

Then, as the evening ended, everyone was invited outside for a firework finale.

'Who has organised all this?' Zoë asked as they made their way out to the entrance hall.

'Lord Stanberry, the owner of the house,' Callum answered as he reached to help Sally with her wrap.

'The name is familiar,' Zoë said with a frown.

'I should think so. He's one of the richest men in the country.' Sally was quick to inform her. 'The parties that he used to throw here were spectacular at one time.'

'Well, this one is pretty good.' Mark laughed.

'Yes, but they used to be better.' Sally insisted. 'At one time it was very select, only the cream of society was invited. Those were the days when there were high standards of course. Not like now when even the domestic help can buy a ticket.'

Zoë recognised the veiled insult, but merely found it amusing. 'Ah, the good old days, when the peasants knew their places,' she agreed sardonically. 'Quite right, Sally, standards are dropping. Back to the workhouses, I say.' She saw the gleam of humour in Callum's eye, but Sally didn't look at all amused. She tossed her dark hair in a disdainful manner and then smiled up at Callum. 'Shall we go outside? We don't want to miss the fireworks.'

'We've had a pretty good display already,' Mark murmured as Sally marched off, her head in the air.

'She's a bit highly-strung, isn't she,' Zoë remarked in a low tone to Mark as they followed the other couple.

'Oh, yes.' Mark nodded. 'Very volatile, by all accounts.'

It was bitterly cold outside. As Zoë stopped to adjust the wrap around her more securely, she was separated from Mark. She continued to walk with the flow of people out to the lawn, thinking she would catch up with him in a moment.

But once down in the garden it was hard to see anyone, there were so many people and it was so dark.

Instead of merging into the crowd, she walked along the edge. Everyone had congregated on the open spaces of the lawn but, further around the house, there was an Italian garden, its fountains and marble statues lit by the twinkle of garden lights.

She was sidetracked by its beauty and walked further into it, admiring the delightful way it was set out, relishing the solitude for a while.

That was where Callum found her a few minutes later, deep in thought as she looked up at the statue of a lion.

'We were starting to get concerned that we'd lost you.'

His deep voice startled her out of her reverie.

'Sorry.' She turned to look up at him. 'I couldn't find you; then I got distracted by this place.'

'So I noticed.' He smiled. 'You seemed miles away. What were you thinking about anyway?'

'I was admiring him.' She placed a hand on the statue of the lion whose powerful body was paused as if about to pounce. 'He's very impressive, don't you think?'

'Yes.' Callum's eyes moved to the animal.

'It reminds me of my father,' she said contemplatively.

Callum's eyebrows rose. 'Why's that?'

'I don't know.' Zoë grinned and turned away from the statue. 'Maybe because Dad has been on my mind a lot recently, or maybe because Dad is a Leo: very bossy, very domineering. Or perhaps it's because he has a statue just like this one in his garden.'

'Must be some garden.'

'It is.' She thought about the formal lawns, the large house with so many rooms that were unused.

'Why are you thinking about your father so much?' Callum asked gently.

'I suppose it's because we've fallen out…'.

'Why?' He waited for her to talk about it, wanting to hear her side of this story.

She shrugged. 'I don't want to bore you with it.'

'I won't be bored if you want to talk about it.' He hesitated before adding, 'Wasn't it you who told me that it helps to talk about things?'

She looked into Callum's eyes and smiled. 'Yes, I did, didn't I? Very forward of me.'

'You're a bit audacious on the quiet,' he agreed with a grin.

She laughed. 'That's just it. I'm not really. I've always tried to toe the line for Dad, always tried to be the dutiful daughter—'

'Except when you nearly got yourself expelled from school,' he interrupted with a grin.

'Bringing that up now is a bit beneath the belt, Callum.' She looked up at him teasingly. 'That was told in the strictest confidence.'

'Don't worry, your misdeeds are safe with me,' he assured her, laughing.

She grinned. Then, suddenly, she was serious again, 'Joking apart though, Callum. I'm twenty-three and Dad just can't let me get on with my life without trying to mould me into something I'm not. He wanted me to go into the family business, but I'm useless with figures; I hate being in an office.'

'Maybe he just wants the best for you,' Callum suggested quietly.

'Oh, there is no doubt about that,' Zoë said quickly. 'But what he thinks is the best and what I think are two entirely different things.' She shook her head. 'I've had two serious boyfriends in my life and he's bought both of them off.

One finished with me and then drove off in a Porsche. The other mysteriously got a top job in Dad's office in Edinburgh.'

'Well, if they took his bribes they can't have been very worthwhile people,' Callum said trying to ignore the stirrings of guilt. 'They certainly can't have cared about you very deeply.'

'No.' Zoë looked down at her hands. 'But I could have worked that out for myself. I didn't need Dad to intervene.'

Callum took hold of her hands in his. They were cold and he rubbed at them absently, trying to warm her up. 'Us Dads are a bit over-protective at times,' he said lightly. 'But we usually do it because we love our children.'

'I know he loves me, and I love him.' Zoë shook her head. 'He just pushes it too far. He can't accept that I'm a grown woman and I want to stand on my own two feet. Our latest conflict is down to the fact that Dad says he has found the perfect husband for me.'

She watched the look of surprise on Callum's face and laughed. 'I know, it's absurd, but that's what he said to me. And when I told him that I could find my own husband, thank you very much, he flew into a rage.'

'Well, that's preposterous!' Callum said shaking his head in astonishment. Francis hadn't said anything like that to him and, if he had, he certainly wouldn't have wanted any part in it. 'Who is this guy?'

'I don't know. I've never even met him. And I don't intend to,' she added grimly.

His eyes moved over the gentle beauty of her face, the sadness in her eyes.

'What about the boyfriend you are seeing at the moment?' he asked. 'Does he know about all this?'

'Matthew? Yes, he knows about it all.' Zoë's features relaxed. 'He thinks it's preposterous as well.'

'Do you think your father will try to buy him off?'

Zoë shrugged. 'I don't know. But he'd be wasting his time to even try. My relationship with Matthew is very different from all the others.'

The fireworks started, the night air was lit with their brilliance for a moment and, distracted, they both looked up into the sky.

Zoë had sounded pretty confident about her boyfriend. Callum frowned. He wondered what Matthew was really like? He agreed with him on one thing, Francis's attitude did seem outrageous. But did he know something about this Matthew guy that Zoë didn't? Zoë's father was many things, but he was nobody's fool. Would he risk wrecking a potentially serious relationship just on a whim? Apart from anything else, Francis wasn't a well man. Maybe it was this fact that had prompted him to think about Zoë's long-term security? All right it was completely absurd trying to arrange a marriage for her, but that still didn't mean he was wrong about Matthew.

Callum frowned. He wondered if she knew how ill her father was. If he should tell her, come clean about this whole charade. Talk to her honestly about it. He really wanted to.

The guilt was starting to eat him alive.

She looked away from the golden light spilling dramatically through the dark velvet sky. 'Anyway, I'm sorry I bored you with all that,' she said softly.

'You didn't bore me.'

'Do you think if I just stand firm on this subject with Dad, he'll realise that he can't play games with my life?' She looked up at him, her eyes wide and trusting, as if she really liked him, as if she was eager for his advice. He imagined the change in her expression when she knew that he was in alliance with her father. She'd be furious, and rightly so. But even so, he felt he should tell her.

'Listen, Zoë, there's something you should know…'

There was a particularly loud bang over their heads and a shower of red light spilled through the air.

She moved closer to him.

'Yes?'

'The thing is…'

'Yes?'

If he told her, what would happen? She'd march back to London and straight into Mr Unsuitable's arms. Callum's mind suddenly galloped ahead. Was that what he wanted? If this Matthew guy was everything her father had said he was, he might not be doing Zoë any favours coming clean.

He looked deep into the beauty of her eyes and summoned a teasing grin. 'The thing is, I don't know if my advice would be particularly helpful as my star sign is Leo, too.'

She laughed.

It wasn't the right time. He consoled himself that he'd done the right thing. She was upset now. He should tell her when she was feeling less torn about her father and more relaxed; less likely to run back to the unsuitable Matthew and maybe just marry him in a fit of pique.

She smiled up at him, her eyes moving over the handsome contours of his face.

'Thanks for trying to cheer me up, Callum,' she said softly. 'And for being a good listener.' She stood on her tiptoes, intending to kiss him on the cheek. It was an impulsive move, one she didn't really think about. But, somehow, instead of finding his cheek, her lips met with his.

The feeling that ignited inside her was more explosive than the fireworks around them. The touch of his lips against hers was sensual and provocative, deeply stirring. She leaned closer, deepened the kiss further, feeling her body pressed close against his, delighting in the sensation.

A voice calling their names made them break apart. They stared at each other wordlessly, both of them breathless.

'There you are.' Mark marched over. He noticed the way they were standing so close together, the way Callum's arm rested lightly at Zoë's waist.

'We've been looking all over for you.' He grinned. 'Sally is spitting feathers.'

The smell of gunpowder hung in the air as the last of the firework rockets exploded above them.

Callum stepped back from Zoë. 'Why is that, then?' he asked calmly.

'Heaven knows.' Mark grinned.

As they turned to follow Mark back towards the crowds, Zoë hung back.

'Are you OK?' Callum asked quietly.

'Yes, of course.' Zoë could hardly bring herself to look at him. The kiss had been wonderful, but she had initiated it and that made her feel incredibly awkward. She wasn't Callum's date tonight, Sally was. She slanted a quick glance over at him. 'Listen, about that kiss,' she said nervously, feeling she should broach the subject before they joined Sally, 'I'm sorry, I was upset…and you were being so kind—'

'Kind?' Callum's eyes narrowed. 'Well, I'm just a real nice guy,' he murmured sarcastically.

Nice didn't even begin to describe how she had felt about Callum during that kiss. Sizzling passion had overwhelmed her senses to the state that, even now, she felt light-headed. 'Yes, you are.' She smiled at him somewhat tremulously, thinking that that had to be the understatement of the year.

# CHAPTER EIGHT

ZOË had just finished making the beds when she heard Callum calling to her up the stairs.

'Coming.' She ran a final, smoothing hand over the duvet before turning to hurry downstairs.

Callum was in the kitchen. 'I didn't expect to see you back so soon,' she said, glancing at the clock. It was ten-thirty Monday morning. She had thought she wouldn't see anyone until she picked the children up from school.

'I've got to go into Windermere to pick up Alice's birthday present.' His eyes moved over the kitchen table. It was groaning with food, most of it home-baked. Iced buns and cakes, gingerbread men, all beckoned invitingly. He reached out and stole a chocolate square.

'Hey!' She reached over to cover the plates with the net covers she had bought earlier. 'The food is for later; hands off.'

'And I thought you said Leo's were bossy.' He grinned over at her. 'It looks very tempting. Can't I just have a cake?'

'No.' She put her hand on her hip. 'You can have some at the party.'

'Spoilsport.' He reached under the net and took one anyway. Munching on it defiantly, he cast a wickedly teasing look over at her.

'Definitely a Leo,' she said with a shake of her head.

'And proud of it.' He dusted his hands on his jeans. 'You look as if you have things pretty much under control here.'

She nodded. 'There was something wrong with the ra-

diator in the bathroom though. I've bled it and I think it's
OK now—'

'You should have let me see to it,' Callum murmured.
'You've got enough to do.'

'No, it's all right. Everything is ready and just waiting
for the birthday girl.'

'Would you like a trip into Windermere with me, then?'

The invitation came as a surprise. 'Well…'

'I could do with some advice with this present.'

'Oh. OK.' She smiled at him, pleased by the invitation.
'I'll just comb my hair and put some lipstick on. I won't
be a moment.'

His gaze moved to the softness of her lips. 'No, don't
be long.'

Something about the husky quality of his voice made her
heart miss a beat. Made her remember the stolen kiss they
had shared the other night.

Zoë frowned. She didn't want to think about that; she
had been trying so hard to act as if it had never happened.
Turning away from him she hurried upstairs.

She studied her reflection in the bedroom mirror. She
was wearing grey trousers with pockets in the side and a
white polo-neck sweater. On impulse, she pulled the jumper
off and changed into a low-scoop-neck top in soft petal
pink. Then she reapplied deep pink to her lips and shook
her hair out of its pony-tail to brush it vigorously. Suddenly
she looked alluring and glamorous. Was it too much for a
casual trip into town with her employer? Maybe she was
showing a bit too much cleavage.

She grabbed a heavy grey fleece out of the wardrobe and
zipped it up. Better, she thought with a nod. She didn't
want to look too provocative.

Callum's eyes moved over her in a comprehensive, assessing sweep as she arrived back in the kitchen, making
her feel incredibly self-conscious.

'Right, ready when you are,' she said breathily as she reached for her handbag.

It was a bright, clear day, not a cloud in the sky. All along the verges of the road golden daffodils fluttered in the breeze. There were swathes of them everywhere, lighting the shadows under the trees, by the lake and in the cottage gardens.

'I love this time of the year.' Zoë smiled. 'Makes me think that summer is just around the corner. Everything ahead suddenly seems golden and full of promise.'

'It's nice to look forward to the summer,' Callum agreed, changing down gears as they descended a steep part of the narrow country road. He glanced across at her. 'What are your plans when you get back to London?' he asked nonchalantly.

She took a deep breath wondering if she should tell him about the art exhibition she was planning. She was superstitious when it came to talking about it, a bit afraid in case it wasn't a success. If all her dreams fell to dust...she'd feel such a fool. Only her closest most trusted friends knew about April the fifteenth.

Hesitantly she started to tell him. 'Well, I'll be taking up my painting again.'

'Not many landscapes to paint in London,' he said wryly.

'That's not true. There are lovely scenes to paint both in and around London; Monet certainly thought so.'

He grinned. 'Well, I suppose there are a few, but it's better here.'

She looked out over the sweep of green fields. A church nestled amidst the folds of green and, behind it, the mountains rose spectacularly. 'I agree, it is an artist's dream up here,' she remarked.

'Yes, a lot of artists and writers have lived up here. Beatrix Potter being one of them. Her house is nearby.' He glanced over at her again. 'So, apart from painting,' he probed, trying to sound casual, 'anything else lined up?'

'Not really.'

Why did he feel she was keeping something from him? he wondered. Hell, he hoped she wasn't planning to elope with the boyfriend. He slowed the car.

Why did he hope so fervently that she wasn't planning to marry? Because it would break her father's heart? Because he liked her and the thought of her being hurt by some charlatanic rogue made his hackles rise? Which was it? Maybe a bit of both, maybe neither. Maybe it was just the basic fact that he found her highly desirable. He couldn't get the memory of that kiss out of his mind. It was driving him crazy.

Up ahead the road came to an abrupt end as it met the lake. A few cars were lined up waiting for the ferry across. Callum pulled up in the queue and switched off the engine.

'Here we are: Lake Windermere,' he said with a smile. 'Bowness is just at the other side on the lake shore, and the town of Windermere is behind it, further up the hill.'

She watched as the ferry made its slow, laborious way across towards them. It was just a small car deck with a covered area for foot passengers at one side. She remembered travelling across here as a child.

It was a picturesque scene: the thickly wooded hills behind the cold blue of the water, yachts and pleasure cruisers bobbling about on the wake of the ferry.

In a little over a week she would be going back to London, Callum thought, turning to look at her. He cleared his throat. 'I know I mentioned it before, but I don't suppose you would reconsider and stay with us a bit longer?'

She looked over at him thoughtfully. 'How long?'

'I don't know, a few months...maybe longer.'

She shook her head. 'I can't Callum—'

'Why? You can paint up here, can't you?' He spread his

hands. 'Look, if it's about spare time then I can let you have space and time to paint. We have a big attic. Now I think about it, it would make an ideal studio. It's airy; there are even picture windows that have incredible views out over the fells.'

She frowned. 'That's really kind of you, Callum.' She was incredibly tempted to just say yes, and very touched by his offer. 'You must think I'm doing a good job with the children.'

'Yes. I like the way you are with them.'

The sincerity in his tone made it all the harder to turn down the offer.

But this job had only ever been meant as temporary. In fact, her time with the agency had only been a means to an end; temporary contracts gave her flexibility to concentrate more spare time on her artwork. She took a deep breath. 'No...I really can't, Callum.'

'I see.'

She watched a muscle flicker at the side of his jaw. She felt he wanted to say more.

The ferry docked in front of them and the ramp lowered, allowing the cars to unload. Callum moved round in his seat and turned the keys in the ignition as the vehicles in front started to drive onto the vessel.

On board a man walked from car to car taking the fare for the short journey. They sat waiting to pay, neither speaking.

She wanted to say, Listen, I've changed my mind and I'll stay. Her thoughts were torn. She really liked the children and had grown very fond of them in a short space of time. She really liked Callum...no, she more than liked him.

Her heart missed a beat as she glanced over at him. He was sorting through some loose change to find the correct fare.

She shouldn't feel this wild attraction to him; it was all wrong. She thought about the party the other night: how understanding he'd been when she had spoken about her father, the way he had kissed her. Then she remembered the drive home and Sally.

They had all gone back to the farmhouse for coffee. Afterwards Mark had offered to drive Sally home. But Callum had said it was out of Mark's way and had insisted on taking Sally home himself.

Zoë had retired to bed, but she had lain awake, turning restlessly for ages, unconsciously listening for the sound of Callum's car returning. Much to her annoyance she didn't know what time he had got back because she had fallen asleep, but she knew it had been late. He could even have been out all night. She had kept telling herself it was none of her business and, yet, the image of Callum and Sally making love had taunted her ever since.

The thought made Zoë feel wretched all over again.

Callum's voice brought her back to the present with a start.

'Sorry?' She stared at him blankly for a moment. 'What did you say?'

'Do you want to get out of the car?'

'May as well.' She nodded and reached for the car handle almost gratefully. She didn't want to think any more about Callum and Sally.

The ferry was underway now. The air was fresh and bracing; it chopped the waves of the lake and made Zoë's hair fly about her face in wild disorder.

They leaned against the railings and looked out across the water. 'It's so beautiful up here,' she murmured, breathing in the fresh air and smiling as she noticed how the ducks were swimming to avoid the craft.

The rigging on nearby yachts made a ringing, musical sound as the wind whistled around them.

'So why go back to London?' he asked suddenly.

'Because I have to.' She looked over at him. 'Because my life is there.'

For a moment she allowed her eyes to move over his face, openly searching, committing his features to memory so that, on some lonely London night, she could conjure him up again in her mind. Think about her answer again, and possibly regret her decision?

She looked away hurriedly. 'But I'm really enjoying the job,' she said briskly. 'Especially this morning,' she added with a grin.

The ferry was getting ready to dock at the other side; drivers were returning to their vehicles. Zoë followed Callum back to the car.

'What are you getting Alice for her birthday?' she asked as he started the engine again.

'A doll's house. I put a deposit on it a couple of weeks ago.'

'She'll be thrilled,' Zoë said and then frowned. 'Why do you need my help?'

He smiled. 'Well, when I got home I wondered if I had chosen the right one. They had two beauties: one was a modern house, the other Victorian. I plumped for the Victorian. I just wanted a second opinion.'

He hoped he sounded convincing. The truth of the matter was he'd wanted her company.

They drove off the ferry and up through Bowness. The small wooden jetties that, in summer, would be a hive of activity were quiet today, just a few ducks and swans wad-dling along the stony banks of the lake before plunging into the cold clear water.

'Is it as you remembered?' Callum asked her.

She smiled. 'Yes, it's still as beautiful,' she remarked looking out over the lake and the unspoilt woodlands be-yond.

They drove away from the water and up the hill. Callum found a parking space and they walked up the steep streets towards the shop he wanted.

Zoë agreed with him immediately when she saw the two doll's houses. 'You've definitely chosen the right one,' she said looking through the windows and then opening the doors. 'Alice will love it.'

As Callum paid for the house a rag-doll caught Zoë's eye. It was very unusual with big blue eyes and a sad smile. It seemed to be crying out to be bought. Impulsively she took it down from the shelf. She'd already bought Alice some hair-slides and a pretty hairbrush. It had been the best of a limited selection at the village shop, but this doll was far more suitable.

Callum frowned as she put it on the counter. 'Don't buy anything for Alice, Zoë. She's got enough.'

'Don't be silly. You can never have enough toys when you're six.'

He smiled and relented. 'OK, but, in return, you must let me take you for lunch.'

She hesitated and then smiled. 'That would be very nice.'

She had expected Callum to take her to one of the many cafés nearby. But instead they got back into the car and he drove her to a hotel overlooking the lake.

It had a spectacular restaurant with a wooden deck area where, in the summer, Zoë imagined, it would be very pleasant to sit in the sun and sip drinks, watching the boats sail past.

As it was still early, it wasn't very busy and they got the best table in a secluded alcove with a wonderful view.

'I know they have a very good vegetarian selection in here,' Callum said as he handed her a menu.

She looked across at him, one eyebrow raised. 'Lots of bean casseroles?' she teased. 'Fancy you knowing that. I wouldn't have thought you'd give a vegetarian selection the briefest glance.'

'Someone mentioned it once.' He opened his own menu with a frown of concentration. In fact, he had asked around just recently to find out where the best vegetarian restaurants were. He'd told himself it might come in handy to know these things sometime.

They placed their orders with the waitress and Callum reached to pour her a glass of wine.

'This is a very pleasant surprise. I didn't expect to be taken out for lunch today.' She smiled at him. 'Thank you.'

He smiled back. She was very attractive, he thought for the umpteenth time. He noticed how the pink top she wore revealed the curves of her figure to perfection. She had the most perfect body. Unsuitable Matthew was one lucky guy, Callum thought irritably.

He pulled his thoughts abruptly away from that direction. 'Well, it's the least I could do after you've gone to so much trouble for Alice's birthday,' he said, trying to sound businesslike as if, by doing so, he could banish the fact that he found her utterly desirable. 'I've never seen so much baking.'

She shook her head. 'I enjoyed doing that.' She transferred her attention to the window, watching how the sun sparkled over the surface of the lake. She wished Callum had wanted to take her out for lunch for reasons other than gratitude. 'Anyway, I was just doing my job. You are paying me.'

She watched someone water-skiing from the back of a speedboat. 'Have you ever tried that?' Callum asked as he followed her gaze.

'Yes, a long time ago, I'm not very good, but I enjoyed it.' She looked back at him. 'What about you?'

He nodded. 'Helen used to enjoy water-skiing. We had a speedboat and went out most weekends in the summer.'

It was the first time he had volunteered any real information about his wife, Zoë noted. She didn't push or question him further, even though she was very intrigued to know more.

Instead, she lifted her glass of wine to her lips. She noticed the far-away expression in his eyes as he looked out of the window, as if he was looking back on another life.

'All seems like a long, long time ago now.' He looked back at her. 'I thought I'd spend the rest of my life with Helen, but we were only married for six years.'

'At least you had six happy years. It's more than a lot of people can say.'

'True.' He smiled. 'And time has healed a lot of the pain. It's just periods like the children's birthdays and Christmas that it suddenly resurfaces. She loved the children so much.'

Zoë felt a lump of emotion in her throat. She reached across the table and covered his hand with her own. She didn't say anything; there were no words that would heal that pain.

They looked into each other's eyes for a moment. He took hold of the hand resting on his and squeezed it gently.

The waitress arrived with their food and they broke apart with a jolt.

Zoë looked down at the delicious starter, guiltily aware that her thoughts, when he had held her hand, had moved from sympathy to desire in the space of a few short seconds.

'Sorry, Zoë, I don't usually talk like this.'

She looked over at him. 'Well, you know what my answer to that is,' she said firmly. 'Anyway, I did bend your ear the other night about my problems. I'd say it's your turn now.'

His lips twisted wryly. 'Have you decided what you are going to do about...your father?' Hell, he'd almost said

Francis. The name had hung precariously on the edge of his lips. And how would he have explained that?

'No.' She shook her head. 'But let's not talk about that.'

Maybe that was a good idea for now, Callum thought, trying to regain his equilibrium.

'Can I ask you a really personal question?' she asked suddenly.

He looked over at her warily. 'Go ahead.'

'What happened to your wife?' When he didn't answer immediately, she slanted a fleeting, investigative look at him to gauge how her question had been received. But it was hard to tell how he was feeling; the dark eyes were impenetrable. 'I'm sorry, maybe I shouldn't have asked,' she said hurriedly.

'No. It's OK. It's certainly not a secret.' He shook his head. 'Helen died in a car crash. It was January and the roads up here can be very treacherous at that time. She hit a patch of black ice on the road and her car veered off and overturned. According to the crash investigators, she wasn't even going very fast. But apparently death would have been instantaneous.' He frowned, his voice husky over the last few words.

'I shouldn't have asked,' she said softly, remorse soaring through her. 'I told myself not to.'

He met her eyes across the table and smiled. 'Let's see…' he murmured in a lighter tone. 'You're impulsive, outspoken, probably a bit stubborn when you want to be.' He narrowed his eyes and pretended to weigh her up very seriously. 'I bet your star sign is Taurus.'

She smiled, relieved that they were on lighter ground. 'Are you trying to tell me that I'm a bull-in-a-china-shop kind of Taurus?'

'Am I right?' His eyebrows shot up in surprise.

'No.' She grinned.

'It would be a miracle if I had been,' he said with a laugh. 'I know nothing about star signs.'

The waitress arrived to take their plates away and serve their main course. Callum topped up Zoë's glass of wine.

'So tell me,' he said as they were left alone again, 'as you seem to be something of an authority on the old lion of the zodiac, do they have any good points, or do you find them all equally irritating?'

'Oh, they have some very good points. They are nearly always very good-looking.' Her eyes moved over the handsome contours of his face. 'They are very charismatic, loyal, funny, outgoing, and they are terrifically passionate.'

'Really?' His lips slanted in an amused smile. 'How do you know all that?'

'Because I am a Leo.' She met his eye with a mocking, challenging glint of mischief. 'How do you think?'

'And I was just starting to feel flattered.' He burst out laughing. It was a deep, velvet, thoroughly amused kind of laugh and she found herself laughing with him. 'You have the self-assurance of a lion, I'll give you that.'

'Thanks.'

They laughed again.

'So, what kind of things do you feel passionate about?' he asked.

'Oh, all kinds of things.' She shrugged. 'Animals, my painting, injustice of any kind and, of course, people I love.'

'Matthew being one of them?' he asked quietly.

She hesitated. 'Yes, Matt is very special to me, but—'

'Zoë, there is something I forgot to tell you,' Callum cut across her feeling miserably guilty. 'Matthew left a message for you on the answering machine, the night of Kyle's concert. I listened to it when I came in and then…well, I was in such a hurry, I didn't get around to telling you.'

'Well, I'm sure if it's important he'll ring back.' Zoë

shrugged. 'Actually I tried to phone him yesterday, but I only got his answering machine. It seems like we're playing phone tag.'

'He said something about April the fifteenth. Just that everything was OK and not to worry. Something like that.'

'Oh.' Zoë nodded. 'Good.' She reached for her glass of wine and finished it.

'So what's happening on the fifteenth?' Callum asked steadily. 'Or shouldn't I ask?'

She took a deep breath. 'I'm holding an art exhibition at one of Matt's studios.' Her eyes shone with excitement as she told him.

'An art exhibition?' he repeated, making sure he had heard correctly.

She nodded. 'My first. I'm a bit nervous about it. Well, actually I'm very nervous.' She grimaced. 'But I've worked really hard and Matthew says he wouldn't be promoting me if he didn't think I stood a chance at becoming successful, so I'm just going with the flow, as they say.'

'An art exhibition!' Callum shook his head. 'Zoë that's marvellous.' If he sounded overenthusiastic, he couldn't help it. He was just so relieved that the fifteenth hadn't turned out to be a wedding date.

'I hope it will be marvellous.' She grinned. 'But I don't know. It's all uncharted territory. I wouldn't have been able to get this far without Matt's encouragement and help.'

'He seems like a decent guy,' Callum ventured.

'The best.' She nodded. 'He's helped me keep my nerve and he's never stopped believing in me.'

Was she in love with him? She seemed very enthusiastic, very taken with him. He wanted to ask, but the question was too personal. Instead, he said nonchalantly, 'I thought when I heard his phone message that the fifteenth might be a wedding date.'

Her eyebrows rose. 'Heavens, no!'

'Does your father know about the exhibition?'

'No—'

The waitress interrupted them. She cleared away the empty plates and asked if they'd like coffee or dessert.

Zoë glanced at her watch. 'I don't think we have time have we, Callum? We don't want to be late picking up the children.'

'No.' Callum looked at his watch. 'You're right. We'd better go.' Regretfully he asked the waitress for the bill. He would have liked to sit for a while longer, probe a bit deeper but, maybe, there would be time for that later.

# CHAPTER NINE

BETWEEN picking up the children and Alice's party, t was a lot to do that afternoon. Zoë was extremely gra when Callum made it clear that he had taken the rest o day off. Apart from the fact that it was helpful to have about whilst sixteen children were hurtling around house, there was also something very comfortable a working alongside him. He had an easy manner. He great fun and just being close to him gave her a thrill was utterly mystifying, yet wonderful.

They laughed together as they blew up balloons, tea each other about being unfit and out of breath. They pl pass-the-parcel with the children. Then, as the chil danced around the living-room to the latest pop album, retired to the kitchen to start organising the food.

'I suddenly feel old.' Callum laughed as he took a d of water from the tap. 'All that leaping up and down nearly finished me off.'

'You're a good dancer though.' Zoë grinned. 'A bit your sell-by date, but not in bad nick.'

'Very funny.' He levelled a teasing look at her. 'I'll you know I'm in my prime.'

'Is that what it is?'

He flicked some cold water from the tap over at her she shrieked as it caught her.

Amidst the laughter the back door opened and S walked in. 'Sorry.' She looked from one to the othe them. 'I did knock on the front door but no one seeme hear.'

'Not surprising with the racket that lot are maki

134

Callum said easily, indicating the loud music in the other room with a nod of his head. 'Come on in. Let me take your coat.'

Sally was wearing the most fabulous cashmere coat and, beneath it, a sheath dress in deep green velvet. She looked stunning. By comparison, Zoë suddenly felt dowdy in her casual trousers and top. But, then, she wasn't here as a guest, she was here to work, she told herself crossly as she slid another batch of sausage rolls out of the oven.

It was crazy to resent Sally's appearance; she had been invited, after all. And she was possibly a very nice person, Zoë told herself crisply as she went over to help her two children with their coats.

Clara was dressed in a full-length velvet dress with a high collar; it made her look like a choirgirl and restricted her movements as she walked. Natalie, the youngest, was wearing a denim pinafore dress. She was a cute child with a wide bright smile, totally unlike her sister.

'Alice is through in the lounge if you'd like to go in,' Zoë said with a smile.

Natalie went rushing off, but Clara stayed behind with the adults.

'Glass of wine Sally?' Callum asked as he uncorked a bottle of white.

'Thanks, that would be nice.' The woman's eyes moved over the food on the table. 'This looks very appetising.'

'Yes, Zoë has worked wonders.'

Sally's gaze moved from the food to Zoë. There was a cosy atmosphere in the kitchen that seemed to have nothing to do with the heat from the Rayburn.

'Turning out to be quite a little asset, aren't you, Zoë?' she said.

The words were spoken jovially, but Zoë was sure that venom lurked not very far beneath the surface.

'I try my best,' Zoë answered with a shrug. Was it her

imagination, or had the happy atmosphere of a few moments ago suddenly fizzled out into something much more serious.

She glanced across at Callum. His eyes were on Sally. No wonder he was looking at her. She had worried about the neckline on her top; it was nothing to the plunging cleavage that Sally was displaying.

Hardly appropriate for a children's party, Zoë thought glumly, then wondered suddenly if she was jealous of the woman's involvement with Callum. The idea was most unpleasant. She had no earthly right to be jealous. But, if she wasn't, why did she have this irrational dislike of the woman? It really wasn't like her at all.

'Glass of lemonade, Clara?' She turned her attention to the child, trying desperately to put her disturbing thoughts to the back of her mind.

'No, thank you.'

Zoë frowned. 'I tell you what, why don't you come into the other room with me? We're going to play musical bumps in a moment.'

The child stared at her blankly. 'You know the game,' Zoë enthused. 'When the music stops you've got to sit down—'

'I know what musical bumps are, silly,' Clara cut across her sharply. 'But I'm too old to play them.'

'Do it, please, Clara. It's Alice's birthday and she loves that game.' Zoë held out her hand. 'Come on, you'll enjoy yourself,' she encouraged.

Reluctantly, Clara allowed herself to be led into the other room.

She was doing the right thing, Zoë told herself as she launched into playing games with the children. She was giving Sally and Callum some time to themselves. Even so, from time to time she glanced towards the door, hoping that they weren't going to be too long on their own.

Contrary to expectations, Clara seemed to thoroughly enjoy herself over the next half hour. When everything was running smoothly and the children were once more just dancing, Zoë returned to the kitchen to bring more food through to the other room. She was surprised to find Sally on her own.

'Callum's gone out to check on one of the horses,' she told Zoë.

'That will be Nell. She's expecting a foal any day.' Zoë poured herself a glass of lemonade.

'When did you say you were leaving, Zoë?' Sally asked her suddenly.

Why was she always asking her that? Zoë wondered irately. 'I don't know.' She shrugged and was deliberately vague. 'I'll have to see how things go.' It was none of Sally's business anyway, she told herself.

'So are you thinking of taking up Callum's offer to stay longer, then?'

Zoë turned to look at the other woman in surprise. 'He told you about that?'

'Yes, of course. Callum tells me everything.' Sally smiled. 'We are quite close, you know.'

'I see.' Zoë busied herself putting food onto trays. She didn't know why she had felt surprised that Callum had told Sally about his offer. She felt a bit foolish now.

'We've had an understanding for quite some time. I suppose it was inevitable that our relationship would deepen,' Sally continued smoothly.

Was she talking about what had happened between them the other night when Callum had taken her home? Zoë really didn't want to hear about this, yet she felt compelled to listen.

Sally gave a light-hearted laugh. 'Yes. If things keep going the way they are, and you stay on much longer, you might end up working for me as well.'

Zoë glanced up at her trying her best not to look as horrified as she felt.

'I'm telling you this strictly in confidence, you understand. Callum isn't ready to announce anything publicly yet.' Sally waved a hand airily. 'As you'll appreciate, he wants to take things slowly with the children, get them used to me gradually. But there is a strong possibility of us getting together on a more permanent basis.' She sighed. 'And with four children between us, I tell you, we'd need your help.'

'Yes, I'm sure you would.' Was that the reason Callum had asked her to stay on? The thought was horrifying. 'But I think I'll be going back to London pretty soon, anyway.' Zoë put the last of the crisps into a bowl hurriedly; she wanted to get out of the room and away from this conversation.

'Pity.' Sally took a sip of her wine and gave her a rather smug look that was anything but regretful.

Zoë headed back into the lounge. She was just in time to see Clara sticking out a foot, tripping Kyle up. The boy had been running after someone and he fell full length on the carpet with a terrible thud.

For a second he just lay there winded and then he started to cry. Zoë put down her tray and hurried over to pick him up.

'Are you OK?' She held him as he tried to choke back his sobs.

'Clara tripped him up,' Alice wailed.

'No, I did not.' Clara put one hand on her hip. 'He was running around like a baby and he fell.'

Zoë thought it best to ignore this. Instead, she concentrated on Kyle. 'Where does it hurt? Did you hit your head?'

'No, my knees are sore.'

Zoë gave them a rub for him. 'Feeling better now?' she asked.

He nodded.

Sally came into the room, her face a picture of concern. 'What's going on?' she asked.

'They said that I tripped Kyle up, but I didn't. He was running around like a silly baby and he fell,' Clara informed her.

'Really, Kyle!' Sally shook her head. 'You're old enough to know better. I think you owe Clara an apology.'

'I do not.' Kyle was very red in the face.

Sally's eyebrows rose. 'I wonder what your dad will say when he hears what a naughty boy you have become.'

Kyle's face tightened and Zoë quickly patted his shoulder reassuringly. 'Oh, I don't think it need come to that. There's no harm done. Let's have lemonade and cut the cake,' she suggested, trying to change the subject.

'I don't want any,' Clara muttered. 'It's horrible. My birthday cake last month was much nicer.'

'No, it wasn't,' Kyle said furiously. 'Zoë baked that cake and it's great.'

'You haven't even tasted it yet so how would you know?' Clara demanded imperiously.

'Now, now, I think perhaps you are all getting a little overexcited, Clara,' Zoë cut in quickly. Her head was starting to throb. She glanced surreptitiously at her watch. Just another half an hour at the most—it seemed like an eternity. 'Come on into the kitchen and we'll get lemonade. Alice put the music back on.'

'Kyle's behaviour is unacceptable,' Sally murmured in an undertone to Zoë as they went into the other room. 'What that boy needs is a mother to sort him out.'

'Well, in fairness to Kyle, I did see Clara trip him up,' Zoë said softly.

Sally's face contorted with anger at that statement. 'I don't think so,' she said coldly.

Zoë was saved from having to make a reply when one of the other children came running in. 'The bathroom has flooded. It's wet all over the floor,' he told Zoë importantly.

Callum walked into the room in the midst of this statement. 'What the heck is happening here?' he murmured taking in Sally's angry stance. 'What's happened in the bathroom?'

'I don't know,' Zoë muttered. 'I hope it's not something I did to the radiator.'

'Well, I did say you should have left that radiator to me,' Callum muttered with a shake of his head as he left the kitchen to investigate.

Zoë caught the pleased smile on Sally's face as she followed him out.

Kyle looked at Zoë and went over and gave her a quick hug. He didn't say anything but, somehow, the gesture touched Zoë deeply.

'Just a quick word, Callum.' Sally caught up with him by the stairs and placed a detaining hand on his arm.

'What is it?'

Sally sighed. 'I know it probably isn't the right time to bring this up, but I just thought you should know—'

'What?'

'Well…I don't quite know how to put this, but Zoë has been very sharp with the children. No patience at all.'

Callum frowned. 'That doesn't sound like Zoë.'

Sally shrugged. 'I'm just telling you what I heard. Also, she was very rude to me and Clara.'

Callum frowned. 'Maybe this isn't the best time to talk about this, Sally.'

'Are you saying you don't believe me?' Sally's tone was tremulous.

Callum's eye flicked from Sally to Alice who had run over towards them and was listening to every word.

'Let's talk about it later, shall we?'

Sally nodded tersely.

In the kitchen Zoë was putting the candles into Alice's birthday cake.

She was surprised when Sally marched back into the room accompanied by both her children and took their coats from behind the door.

'Are you leaving Sally—?'

'I certainly am.'

Without a backward glance they disappeared slamming the door behind them.

'Well, they weren't a lot of help, were they,' Zoë murmured to Kyle with a grin.

When the back door opened again, Zoë thought, for one awful moment, they had come back. She was relieved to see Callum's mother, closely followed by Mark.

'Where's the birthday girl?' Ellen called and Alice came running from the other room to fling herself at her grandma with a big hug.

'Happy birthday, darling,' Ellen said. 'Are you having a good time?'

'It's great, best party ever,' Alice enthused. 'I got a doll's house. Oh, and Zoë flooded the house and Sally said Zoë was rude to her,' Alice repeated her story with glee. 'I heard her telling Daddy in the lounge.'

'Really?' Both Ellen and Mark looked over at Zoë making her feel very uncomfortable.

Ellen grinned over at Zoë. 'Well, sounds eventful at any rate.'

'It's a bit of an exaggeration, Ellen,' Zoë said, trying to sound cheerful.

'Actually it's a lot of an exaggeration,' Callum put in from the doorway behind them. 'Zoë hasn't flooded the house. Someone has put the plug in the washbasin and left the tap running. The bathroom is a bit wet, but it will dry out.'

Although Zoë was relieved to discover she wasn't to blame for the flood, her relief was tinged with the sharp feeling of distress that he hadn't disputed the other part of Alice's statement. He could at least have stuck up for her until he heard her side of the story. But, then, he would take his girlfriend's side, she supposed gloomily.

A roll of thunder split the air. Zoë finished putting the last of the dishes into the dishwasher and looked out of the kitchen window. The night sky was illuminated suddenly with the distant flash of lightning. A storm was rolling in over the mountains and the air was heavy and tense with it.

Callum was out in the stables with Mark, had been for the last hour as, just after the drama of the flood, Nell had given birth to her foal. Ellen was upstairs reading bedtime stories to the children, who showed no signs of sleepiness even after all the day's excitement.

Zoë poured two cups of tea and carried them outside for the men. The night was surprisingly warm, perhaps because of the storm. The air was almost muggy.

A paraffin lamp dimly lighted the stable. By its flickering light Zoë could see the newborn foal was on its feet, shaky and vulnerable but beautiful.

'Just in time to welcome the new arrival,' Callum said with a grin. 'Mother and child are doing well.'

'That's wonderful.' Zoë handed them the mugs of tea, then went over to have a closer look.

'I'll be off now, Callum,' Mark said briskly as he finished the drink in one gulp.

'Is Mum going with you?' Callum asked.

'No, she drove here herself.'

'I took her a cup of tea little while ago,' Zoë told them, 'She's reading to the children.'

'At that rate, she'll be up there for the night.' Mark laughed.

'Thanks for your help,' Callum said, walking to the door with him. 'Sorry you didn't get to play musical bumps at the party.'

'Just my luck!' Mark grinned. Then, with a wave at Zoë, he left them.

Zoë stroked the foal's soft velvety coat. 'She's lovely, Callum. What are you going to call her?'

'I don't know.' Callum grinned. 'Flood Alert? Storm Approaching? What do you suggest?'

'It's up to you.' Zoë shrugged.

'Zoë's Disaster?'

She frowned. 'The flood wasn't my fault, remember?'

'Yes, but you thought it was.'

'No, you thought it was.'

He grinned.

'Oh, you're all smiles now, but earlier you were glaring at me as if I'd done something terrible.'

'No, I wasn't.' He sipped his tea and sat down on a bale of hay, his eyes flicking over her slender figure. Something about the way he looked at her made her heartbeats increase.

'I was agitated,' Callum admitted. 'I had a horse in the throes of labour, I had a flooded bathroom, and Sally ranting at me like something demented. It's little wonder I was a bit on edge.'

The mention of Sally's name made Zoë feel more than a little on edge herself.

'Anyway...' he grinned at her again '...all's well that ends well.'

'Is that what you call it?'

He frowned. 'Nell's happy. The bathroom will dry out.

I'll sort Sally out: go and see her tomorrow and smooth things over. The children were happy. The horse giving birth was a lovely excitement for them, sort of rounded off the birthday party.' He shrugged. 'What more could we want?'

Zoë stared at him. 'When you go around to see Sally, are you going to apologise on my behalf?'

'No, of course not.'

'I wasn't rude to her, Callum. I was just sticking up for Kyle,' she told him heatedly.

'Yes, he told me you were nice to him,' Callum said gently.

'Did he?' She was taken aback.

He nodded. 'When he was out here seeing the foal.'

'Oh…' The fire of annoyance died down somewhat.

'Don't worry about Sally. She's got a bad temper, but I don't think she really means it. She's just highly-strung. I'll calm her down tomorrow.'

How was he going to do that? Zoë wondered. She imagined him taking the other woman into his arms, kissing her. The image made her feel wretched. She pushed a hand through the length of her blonde hair, willing herself not to think like that.

'Come and sit down,' Callum said, pulling out a bale of hay next to him. 'You look tired.'

'I am a bit,' she admitted. 'Must have been those two glasses of wine at lunch.'

'Lunch seems like a very long time ago,' Callum said as he finished his drink and put the cup down.

'Yes…' She thought about their time together. 'I enjoyed it very much though.'

'So did I,' he said quietly. 'Maybe we could do it again sometime soon?'

'It will have to be sooner rather than later. I'll be going back to London next week.'

'The kids will be upset.'

'Do you think so?'

'I know so.'

She would have liked to ask whether he would miss her, but that was overstepping the mark, she supposed. Anyway, of course he wouldn't: she was just an employee, easily replaced. The thought was a bit depressing.

She sighed. 'I must admit, I'll miss them.'

She remembered the way the four of them had laughed together as they'd played those silly party games, the look on Alice's face as she'd opened up her birthday presents and the way Kyle had hugged her in the kitchen.

For a brief spell of time, Zoë had felt as if she really belonged here. It was a crazy feeling when she had been here so short a time, even crazier when she took Sally into the equation.

'Then, don't go,' he said softly.

She met his dark eyes and, for a moment, hesitated. Then she remembered Sally telling her if she stayed long enough she would be working for her as well. The notion was appalling. 'I told you, Callum. I can't. This was only ever meant to be a temporary job. Besides, I've got an art exhibition to see to.'

She walked across and sat down next to him. The fresh hay smelt sweet like a summer's day. Nell was licking her new foal, nudging her gently. It was a tender scene in the flickering lamplight.

'I should have brought my sketch pad out here,' she remarked quietly. 'This would have made a good study.'

'Well, it's your day off tomorrow, you can come out here and have a go.' He glanced over at her. 'You'll have to show me some of your work. I'd be really interested.'

She smiled. 'I'd invite you to my exhibition, but I think it would be a bit far for you to travel.'

'Where is it being held?'

'Matt's studio on the Embankment. It's call Devine Art, because of his name, you know, Matthew Devine.'

'That's a name and a half,' Callum said sarcastically. 'Is it for real?'

'Yes, it is.'

'Do you think you can trust him?' Callum asked suddenly, remembering how Francis had described him as a petty crook and confidence trickster. 'I mean the name sounds a bit dodgy to me.'

'What do you mean a bit dodgy?'

'Matthew Devine,' Callum drawled. 'Can you really trust a man called divine?'

'It's spelt with an E.'

Callum ignored this. 'Has he taken money from you for this exhibition?' he asked suddenly.

'You know, you're starting to sound like my father,' Zoë said warily.

'I thought you said your father didn't know about the exhibition?'

'He doesn't. But if he did, I'm sure that's the kind of question he'd ask. He doesn't have any faith in my talents either.'

'I didn't say I hadn't any faith in your talents,' Callum said quickly. 'I just said—'

'I know what you said, I heard you.' Zoë started to get up from the hay, but he reached out a hand and pulled her back down beside him.

'I'm sorry. I didn't mean it to sound like that. But, from what you've told me, your father's a wealthy guy, how can you be sure that this Devine character doesn't know that?'

'Because I know Matt. Anyway, he's a wealthy guy himself; he doesn't need my money.'

'How do you know?'

Her eyes narrowed on him. 'You're very suspicious. Are you this cynical about everything?'

'I'm not cynical.' Maybe suspicious, but not cynical, he thought wryly. And if he was suspicious, it was because of what Francis had told him about this Devine character being a con man.

His eyes moved gently over her face. 'I just wouldn't like to see you get hurt, that's all,' he said softly.

'I wouldn't like to see you get hurt either, but I'm not telling you that I think Sally is interested in you, but not your children. That, in all probability, she'd make a lousy stepmother,' Zoë said heatedly. 'I wouldn't dream of being that insensitive.'

'Wouldn't you?' His eyes moved over her face with some amusement.

'No.' She glared at him, her green eyes glowing with fire.

'So, what kind of woman do you think would make a good stepmother for my children?' he asked quietly, his eyes lingering now on her lips.

'I don't know.' Her temper was fading now as quickly as it had risen, her temperature increasing suddenly in a completely different way as she noticed how close he was sitting to her. 'I...I just know that she doesn't seem very warm towards Kyle. And he needs someone understanding...' She tried very hard to concentrate on what she was saying but she was finding it impossible.

He reached out and touched her face. 'Thanks.'

'What for?' Her heart was skipping and beating as if it was a drum doing a solo performance all of its own.

'For caring.' He leaned closer.

Was he going to kiss her? She wanted him to so much it hurt.

'And you're right, Sally would be the wrong choice as stepmother for my children. But I can assure you, I have never even contemplated her for that post.'

'Haven't you?' Her heart was speeding up even more now. 'She sort of gave the impression that you had.'

'Well, I don't know where she got that idea from. You must have misunderstood.'

His voice was very low and husky. 'If I was to think in the long term, I'd need someone very different from Sally around here.'

He was still extremely close, his lips a tantalising space from hers.

'I mean, she'd be useless as a farmer's wife, wouldn't she? Could you see Sally riding out to fix the stone walls, feeding the lambs and generally keeping my house in order?'

She stared at him for a moment, then realised he was teasing her.

'Very amusing, Callum.' She leaned back from him, trying not to feel disappointed. 'But I was thinking about the children's needs, not yours.'

'Ah, well, if we are to get onto my needs...' He leaned over towards her again and she leaned back and, suddenly, they were overbalancing landing with a jolt in the soft hay behind.

Zoë laughed breathlessly as she found herself lying full-length, cushioned in straw, staring up into Callum's eyes. 'How did that happen?'

'No idea but, as tumbles go, it was extremely pleasant.' He grinned at her.

She was suddenly very conscious of the full force of his body pressed against hers.

He made no attempt to move, his body pinning hers under his, his eyes moving over her features—the softness of her lips, the sparkle of her wide green eyes, her blonde hair in wild disarray around her face...

'Now, what were we talking about?' he murmured teasingly. 'Something to do with my needs?'

Before she could answer him, he lowered his head and kissed her.

It was a sweetly searing caress, and it brought a feverish feeling of need flooding through Zoë. For a moment, she tried to control herself and not respond. Then, before she knew what she was doing, she was kissing him back, her heart somersaulting as his arms wrapped themselves around her.

His lips were gently skilled as they moved over hers, arousing her in the most basic way.

Outside, there was another low growl of thunder; it seemed to echo the fierce need inside Zoë. She pressed herself closer to him, wanting him to touch her body, caress her and quench her desire.

'That felt so good,' he murmured as he pulled back.

She swallowed hard, tried to think sensible thoughts, banish the need she felt. But nothing sensible came to mind.

'I want you, Zoë. Desire for you is eating me away...has been from practically the first moment I saw you,' he murmured huskily.

She wondered if he could feel her heart thundering against his. 'Be serious, Callum,' she said quietly. 'This is crazy.'

'Maybe,' he said, looking deep into her eyes. 'But I've never felt more serious.'

And the frightening thing was, neither had she.

She groaned as his hands touched her breasts, caressing them through the thin material of her top.

He lowered his head and kissed her again. This time his lips were firm, masterful, intensely sensual.

'Tell me you want me, too,' he murmured when he lifted his head and looked into her eyes again. His voice was almost a growl; it was accompanied by the thunder outside, purring through the night air like a lion ready to pounce.

She could hardly speak for the tremor inside. 'Want' was

far too mild a word for what he had stirred to life inside her.

He frowned and seemed ready to pull away from her. 'Zoë, tell me I'm not imagining this. You can't kiss me like that and not feel what I'm feeling, surely?'

She smiled then and lifted one hand to stroke it down the side of his face. 'You're not imagining it,' she whispered softly.

Their eyes held for a moment of extreme intimacy. Then he lowered his head and kissed her again. She moaned as he left her lips and traced a teasing line of kisses down her neck. His hands were pulling up her top, caressing her skin, finding her bra and pushing it back until his hands touched the satin softness of naked flesh.

Her breath caught in a gasp of ecstasy as he stroked her with gentle, skilfully pleasurable movements. Then he moved down and his lips traced where his fingers had played a few minutes before.

She stretched her arms above her head, her nipples hard and so sensitive that she wanted to cry out with the desire of needing more.

Then his lips moved lower, kissing the flat planes of her stomach. She felt strangely detached from any rational thought. She felt his hand resting on the buttons of her trousers.

Another low roar of thunder was the only sound between them. Then the rain started, intense and drumming in a musical way on the flat roof of the stable.

The paraffin lamp flickered as a draught caught it. The horses stirred uneasily behind them.

Callum sat up and looked down at her. Her breasts were round and ripe, her ribcage narrow and her stomach flat. His eyes moved to the silver buttons on her trousers. He felt the tight knot of desire throb inside him as he fought against unfastening them.

But how could he make love to her when he hadn't been entirely honest with her? Wasn't that dishonesty being taken to an even higher, more hurtful level if he went ahead now?

He raked a hand through his hair. He didn't want to think about this, he wanted to continue without concern, but his principles were suddenly alive and kicking. He couldn't continue, not until he'd told her the truth.

Hail was showering against the building in an over-whelmingly noisy way.

'We should go back inside,' he murmured.

She sat up, her hair tumbling wildly around her shoulders. She looked like a siren. It took all his efforts of self-control to stop from reaching out to touch her again.

He noticed how her hands were shaking as she reached to cover herself up. 'Yes, you're right.' She didn't look at him as she spoke. She was confused; he could hear it in her voice. It was no wonder. One moment he had been so sure, driven by desire and need, not one care, not one voice of caution and then suddenly...an attack of conscience.

'Zoë, I still want you. I just think we should take things...' His voice was drowned out by the fierce roar of thunder, a noise that made the horses move anxiously.

Callum got up and went over to check on the animals. When he turned back, the stable door was open and Zoë had gone, running through the rain towards the lights of the house.

# CHAPTER TEN

Zoë was in the kitchen trying to dry herself with a hand towel when Callum followed her in.

'Are you OK?' he asked, his voice deep with concern.

'Of course I'm OK.' She didn't look at him, couldn't bring herself to meet his eyes. She sensed him moving towards her and her breathing felt raw and restricted in her throat. 'Why shouldn't I be?' she managed to ask flippantly.

'Because one minute we were making love and the next—'

'And the next, common sense returned,' she finished for him. 'I'm glad it did…honestly I am.' She rubbed at her hair fiercely, unsure whether her anger was driven by hurt pride because he had been the one to pull back from her, or whether she really meant those words. 'It was crazy. A moment of madness.' Of course it was madness she assured herself heatedly. She had never gone in for casual sex in her life and what more could it have been?

'Who are you trying to convince, yourself or me?' There was a note of lazy amusement in his tone.

She glanced up at him sharply and then wished she hadn't as their eyes met and her stomach contracted with a fierce surge of renewed desire.

He had no right to stand there looking so cool, so nonchalant, so…damn blasted handsome when her body was in total chaos. 'I'm not trying to convince anybody,' she snapped. 'I'm just stating a fact.'

'A moment of madness maybe, but an utterly magnificent madness.' His eyes moved from her face to the gentle curves of her body. Her top was damp and he could see

152

the outline of her body clearly. It caused him to have a severe pang of regret that they weren't still out there, rolling together in the hay.

'I still want you, Zoë,' he murmured.

She dropped the towel on the floor. 'Stop it.' Her voice trembled and she put her hands to her ears in an attempt to blot out what he was saying, like a child. 'I'm not listening to this.'

He came closer and took her hands in his, drawing them down from her face. 'I still want you,' he said clearly and decisively.

She felt confused suddenly and vulnerable.

Then he lowered his head and kissed her again. The sweetness of that caress blew all other thoughts away. She felt his hands caressing her through the dampness of her clothes, felt her breasts harden and ache with desire. Then he was pulling up her T-shirt and caressing her with a feverish need that she could only surrender to completely, kissing him hungrily, pressing herself closer, responding with a wantonness that she couldn't even begin to understand.

'You feel so good,' he murmured. 'You have a body that turns me on just looking at it.' The words were peppered with fiercely passionate kisses. 'I want to make love to you completely, right now.'

Through a misty haze of unreality she heard Ellen's footsteps coming downstairs.

They pulled apart hurriedly, Zoë trying to adjust her clothing with hands that trembled. She didn't know whether to feel relieved or disappointed. In fact she was so bemused by her feelings that she couldn't think straight at all.

'You've got straw in your hair,' Callum murmured with a grin, hastily removing it for her.

She felt herself blush as their eyes met.

She still wanted him. The desire he had kindled wouldn't

go away. She had never before felt such an overwhelming desire, a desire that blotted out everything. If they hadn't been interrupted she would have given herself to him freely and without reserve, right here in the kitchen.

He smiled and his fingertips brushed against the rain-drop-dampness of her cheeks in a tender gesture that made her heart twist.

She loved him, she realised suddenly—loved him deeply, completely and utterly.

The shock of those feelings rooted her to the spot, and she stared at him in a kind of disbelief.

Ellen came bustling into the room and Zoë hastily turned away from Callum, picking up the towel at her feet and trying to summon a smile for the other woman.

'The children are both asleep, bless them,' Ellen said. 'Totally worn out by all that excitement.'

Zoë turned to put the kettle on. When you don't know what to do, where to put yourself, make a cup of tea, she mocked herself wryly. 'Would you like a drink, Ellen?' she asked.

'No. I'm going to get off now,' Ellen said, going to get her coat from the hook behind the door.

Part of Zoë wanted to say, 'No, please don't go! Stay, act as a buffer for me, cover this awkward feeling of total bizarre unreality.'

'By the way, there was a phone call for you, Zoë,' Ellen continued nonchalantly. 'Someone called Matthew. He said, would you ring him back in the morning, first thing. He was just on his way out.'

'Oh, OK.' Zoë took some cups out from the cupboard.

She wondered if it was her imagination, but she felt Callum's eyes boring into her back.

'Everything went all right in the stables, I take it?' Ellen asked casually.

Zoë waited for Callum to answer and was so busy concentrating on his answer that she accidentally missed the counter top and a china mug slipped from her hands, smashing on the stone floor.

'Yes, everything went fine, Ellen,' Callum answered calmly, stepping across to pick up the pieces for her. 'The foal is gorgeous. Do you want to take a look before you go?'

The light-hearted conversation went on over Zoë's head. She found it hard to concentrate. How could Callum act so coolly, as if nothing had happened? Maybe, to him, it had meant nothing. Some people saw these things differently, she supposed. Sex for her was a significant step in a relationship, but Callum might regard it as a meaningless, quick fling.

Suddenly she just wanted to get away to the privacy of her bedroom and think. Maybe she didn't love Callum; it could be just an infatuation, she told herself crossly.

Yet, as she turned and their eyes met and she remembered again the heat of their earlier exchange, she knew that it was true. Of course, she loved him; she couldn't have made love like that if she wasn't totally besotted.

'You OK, Zoë?' Ellen asked suddenly, her eyes moving over the girl's pallor with concern.

'Yes, fine.' She smiled.

'You did a wonderful job with the party; Alice really enjoyed herself.'

The party felt as if it had taken place on another planet, Zoë felt so far removed from it now.

'And I like what you've done with the lounge,' Ellen continued.

'The lounge?'

'Yes, you've moved the furniture around. It looks better.'

The normal conversation felt unreal. She glanced over at Callum and then wished she hadn't as their eyes clashed directly before hers skidded away again.

What was he thinking? Probably that she looked a total mess: her hair must be all over the place: her clothes damp and rumpled. She cringed.

'I'll drive you home, Ellen,' Callum offered suddenly, turning to look out of the window. The rain was still torrential and, every now and then, the sky was lit with fork lightning. 'Leave your car here, I'll drop it off in the morning for you.'

'Don't be silly, Callum, I'll be fine—'

'No, you won't,' he cut across her firmly. 'I'll just go and get my car keys.'

Ellen raised her eyebrows at Zoë as they were left alone. 'He does fuss sometimes.'

'Well, the weather does look very inclement. I suppose the roads will be awash with that rain,' Zoë said softly.

Ellen sighed and buttoned up her coat. 'As I was saying, Zoë, the furniture looks very good like that. Now, if you could just persuade Callum that he needs to redecorate in there, you'd really have worked miracles.'

'I think that might be a bit out of my province,' Zoë said with a shake of her head. 'I am only here to look after the children and clear up, not tell him about the decor in the house.'

'Rubbish.' Ellen looked over at her then, a teasing gleam in her eye. 'You must think I'm very naive.'

'Sorry?' Zoë tried not to blush. Did Ellen guess that there was something deeper going on here between her and Callum?

Ellen shook her head and reached out to pat Zoë's hand. 'See if you can talk him into redecorating,' she reiterated. 'He'll listen to you.'

Zoë gave a lopsided smile. 'I don't know where you got that idea from.'

'You're a good influence, Zoë. This house has suddenly felt like a home again since you arrived.'

A movement in the doorway made them both look around. Callum was standing there, his keys in his hand.

How long had he been listening? Zoë wondered, feeling very uncomfortable. He'd think she was conspiring with his mother. Crikey, he might even think she was the sort of woman to read too much into what had happened between them.

A kiss and a cuddle and she was starting to talk about redecorating his house and taking over his life!

'Ready when you are, Ellen,' he said crisply.

He did think that! She just knew it when she heard that serious note in his voice.

As soon as the door closed behind the two of them, Zoë forgot all about the pretence of making tea and ran upstairs.

She paused outside Alice's door. The little girl was warmly tucked up, her rag-doll beside her. Kyle was also fast asleep, his arms out of the covers, his face flushed. She went further into the room and tucked him up before going through to her bedroom.

Her reflection in the wardrobe mirror was not reassuring. She looked like a waif dragged in from the storm. Quickly she took off her clothes and put on her dressing gown before going down to the bathroom for a shower.

Hot water pummelling down over her naked body restored some semblance of sanity.

OK, she was in love with Callum; stoically she tried to accept what had been staring her in the face for days. It explained why her body had behaved so strangely every time he touched her even accidentally. It explained why she had felt so jealous of Sally. The woman's very name made apprehension return. What were Callum's real feelings for her?

She stepped out of the shower and dried herself briskly. She wasn't going to think about Sally; she was going to try to work out where she should go from here. Putting on her dressing gown, she went back to the bedroom and sat at the dressing table to dry her hair.

She'd almost finished when she heard Callum's footsteps in the hallway. Suddenly her mouth felt dry; her heart was racing again.

'Honestly, you're behaving like a teenager,' she told herself crossly. 'He's just a man, like any other man.'

She turned off the hairdryer, sprayed herself with some perfume and sat waiting.

What was she waiting for? she asked herself. What did she want?

She heard the sound of the shower in the bathroom, then the shrill ring of the phone in the hall.

Frowning, Zoë got up and went to answer it.

It was Sally, her voice brisk and very unfriendly as she asked to speak with Callum.

'He's in the shower,' Zoë told her.

'Well, will you tell him that the supper on Friday is—?'

'Hold on a moment.' Abruptly Zoë put the receiver down and went back upstairs to knock on the bathroom door. 'Your girlfriend is on the phone,' she called, a tight feeling of anger in her tone.

She didn't expect the door to open and was completely taken aback when Callum appeared wearing nothing but a towel around his waist.

'What did you say?' he asked.

'Your girlfriend is on the phone.' With difficulty, she drew her eyes away from his chest. He had the most wonderful physique.

The dark eyes held a gleam of amusement as they met hers. 'Who could that be?'

'Don't be obtuse, Callum,' she snapped. 'You know damn well I'm talking about Sally. And while we are on the subject, I'd just like to tell you, I think you are a total cad, going out with her and coming on to me.'

His eyebrows rose at that. 'What about you and Matt?' he drawled sardonically. 'Or doesn't Mr Divine count?'

'Just leave Matt out of this,' she said furiously.

'Why?' he asked calmly.

'Because he has nothing to do with it.'

'That's not strictly true, though, is it?' Callum asked with infuriating calm. 'Aren't you being a bit hypocritical throwing Sally at me like that when you have a boyfriend waiting for you in London.'

'For your information Matt is not a serious boyfriend, he's just a friend.' Zoë said, her voice shaky.

'Really?' Callum smiled.

'Yes, really, so you can stop having a cheap shot at his expense. I'll have you know that at least Matthew is true to his women once he's dating them.'

'And how do you know that?' Callum said dryly. 'Got a crystal ball, have you?'

Her eyes narrowed. 'You know, I don't think you are a very nice person,' she grated suddenly.

'That's not what your lips were telling me earlier.'

She stepped back, restraining a sudden urge to smack his smug face. What was the matter with her? she wondered through the haze of pure white-hot heat. 'Your girlfriend is waiting,' she reiterated. 'And, before I forget, I'm going to have to leave sooner than we had arranged.' She hadn't intended to say that. It just exploded from her in a spur-of-the-moment rush of reckless antagonism.

'What?'

She watched his dark eyes widen and got a curious sense of satisfaction from it.

'You can't leave earlier; we've got a contract.'

'I haven't signed anything.' Zoë turned away from him and into her bedroom. 'I'm going first thing tomorrow morning.'

She sat back at the dressing table. Now, why had she said that? She didn't want to leave.

From downstairs, she could hear the low murmur of Callum's voice on the phone and, all of a sudden, she knew why she had said she would leave tomorrow. Self-preservation. She was jealous, eaten alive with it.

Callum was dating Sally. It was right that she should leave. Being in love with him and living under the same roof was an untenable situation. If she didn't leave, and leave quickly, she was going to lose every scrap of dignity and pride she had.

A light knock on her door caused her nerves to stretch.

'Go away,' she called, trying very hard to remain strong.

Instead of doing as she had asked, Callum turned the handle and walked in.

She noticed that he had thrown on a pair of chinos and a shirt, which he hadn't buttoned up properly. She could see the dark hairs on his chest. She turned away and pretended to be busy at the dressing table.

'I told you to go away,' she said crisply.

'I don't want to go away, and I don't want you to go away,' he said quietly.

She lifted up her hairbrush and ran it through her hair, but her attention was fixed solely on Callum. She could see him in the mirror. She watched warily as he came closer.

'I bet your girlfriend wouldn't be too pleased to hear that. Especially after the run in we had this evening. Wasn't she phoning to tell you to sack me?'

'No!' Callum grated exasperatedly. 'Of course she wasn't. It's none of her damn business anyway.'

Zoë shot him a look of scepticism and continued to draw the brush through her hair.

He came closer and leaned over to take it out of her hand. The contact of his skin against hers made her pull away abruptly as if she had been burnt.

Calmly he put the brush down and then, placing his hands on her shoulder, he turned her to face him, crouching down so that their eyes were level.

'Please don't leave tomorrow, Zoë,' he said, holding her gaze steadily.

'Give me one good reason why I should stay?' she asked, her heart somewhere in her throat.

'Because of this…' He reached and kissed her lips a light caress that was teasingly provocative. 'And because I can't bear to think of life here without you.'

She wanted to melt against him, reach to kiss him again. But she forced herself not to. 'I can't be the third person in some relationship triangle if you are seeing Sally—'

'She was one date, Zoë.' He shook his head. 'And I never led her to believe it was anything more than friendship, I swear.' He raised his hands, cupping her face gently so that she was forced to look at him. The darkness of his eyes was filled with a sweet urgency that tore at her heart.

'What about this supper she was talking about on the phone? Isn't that classed as another date?'

'She was talking about a school fund-raising event. I'm not going to go. I'm not interested in Sally,' he said firmly. 'I'm interested in you. I want you to stay, Zoë.'

She smiled, her resistance dissolving in a wave of pure happiness. He really wanted her. The knowledge was gloriously exhilarating.

He smiled back. 'Of course, if you stay, I'll have to promote you.'

'To what, interior designer?' Her eyes sparkled with mischief for a moment. 'Or have you a different position in mind for me?'

'I've got a few positions in mind for you, if you must know.' He leaned forward and kissed her on the lips again; this time it was a long and seductively sweet kiss.

She was breathless when he pulled back, her heart racing against her chest. 'Tell me more,' she murmured huskily.

'Well, the main position of course, is that of lover and confidante,' he murmured huskily, reaching and sealing the words with another kiss. 'Closely followed by the eminent title of stepmum.'

Zoë pulled back from him, her eyes widening with shock. 'What did you say?'

'I want you to marry me, Zoë,' he said calmly.

She didn't know what to say, she was so totally and utterly taken by surprise.

'I know you'll need time to think,' he said quickly. 'I know I've kind of sprung this on you…but, the more I think about it, the more sense it makes. Ellen was right when she said this house feels like a home again now that you are here. The children like you…I really…really like you.' He lowered his voice to a teasing grin, then reached and kissed her again.

Her head and her heart were reeling as he pulled away again; her lips tingled from the heat of his kiss; her body felt heavy with desire.

An illuminating flash of lightning lit the room and outside a roar of thunder ripped violently through the air. 'There is a chemistry between us, Zoë. I've felt it from the first moment we met. We're right for each other.' He kissed her again, this time with a hunger that made her feel weak inside. She kissed him back, wrapping her arms around his neck.

'So, when did you decide this?' she asked breathlessly as they pulled apart.

'What? That we should get married?' He grinned. 'About twenty minutes ago, when you said you were leaving.'

Her eyebrows lifted.

'I've always been the impulsive type.' His hand moved to the belt on her dressing gown.

'Have you ever heard the old saying, marry in haste, repent at leisure?' she asked, smiling.

'We could have a long engagement if you want.' His hand toyed with the silk belt of her gown. 'So, what do you say? Will you give my proposal some serious thought?'

'I don't know,' she murmured teasingly. 'Are you properly down on one knee?' She bent her head trying to see.

'I'm on both knees. I'm doing nothing by half.' He grinned. 'I'd put a red rose between my teeth and serenade you with a violin if I thought it would work.'

Her eyes moved over his features, noting the laughter in his dark eyes, the tiny lines that fanned out beside them and the sensual curve of his lips. She reached out and touched his lips. 'I'd settle for a simple, "I love you,"' she told him gently.

The laughter died from his dark eyes. There was a moment's hesitation. The room was lit by a series of lightning flashes that seemed to accompany the rapid thud of Zoë's heart as she waited for his answer.

'I love you, Zoë,' he said huskily, his words almost drowned out by the roar of the storm outside.

She smiled and reached to kiss him. 'In that case,' she whispered against his lips, 'I'd be honoured to become your wife.'

He pulled her into his arms and kissed her. The next moment they were both falling down onto the carpet, rolling into each other arms, kissing each other with unreserved desire.

The belt of her dressing gown was discarded, her naked body pressed against him.

He ran his hands over her, gently exploring and caressing her, touching the soft firm swell of her breasts.

'What are we doing down here when there's a perfectly good bed over there?' she asked, whispering the words against his ear, kissing him at the same time.

'Zoë Bernard, are you trying to seduce me?' he murmured, his voice husky with desire.

'Damn right I am.' With a smile, she pulled away from him and stood up, allowing her dressing gown to slip to the floor. 'Am I succeeding?' she asked.

He got to his feet, his eyes moving over her naked figure with unreserved appreciation. 'Absolutely.'

They lay wrapped in each other's arms in the deep comfort of the double bed. Zoë had never known that making love could be this wonderful. She felt a sense of completeness that she had never experienced before, as if she had found her rightful place in life, right here with this man.

Her head was resting against his chest; she could hear the steady beat of his heart as it returned to normal after the vigorously passionate lovemaking.

'You were very good at that,' she said with a smile.

He laughed, the deep rumble vibrating against her ear. 'So were you.' He kissed the top of her head. 'Do you want to do it again?'

'You're not serious?' She rolled over on top of him, looking down into his face with a smile. 'Aren't you exhausted?'

'Do I feel exhausted?'

She kissed him, loving the feel of their bodies pressed so closely together, his hands trailing tenderly down her back.

'I want to make you so happy, Zoë,' he whispered.

'Mmm…you are,' she groaned.

'I mean, other than sensually.' He kissed her neck.

'Mmm…' She couldn't concentrate on anything other than the pleasure his body was giving her.

'Zoë, listen to me. There's something I need to say to you.'

'Callum, not now…I'm trying to concentrate.'

'Concentrate?'

'Mmm…'

He laughed and moved with more urgency against her. 'How's the concentration going?' His voice was deep and husky against her ear.

'Don't make me laugh…' she gasped.

He turned, bringing her around with him so that their positions were reversed and he was looking down at her and completely in control. He was a skilled lover, his movements slower, more leisurely than the earlier frantic need as he focused solely on pleasing her, bringing her once more into a state of complete and utter ecstasy.

As she gasped his name and he moved away, they lay apart for a few moments, each trying to catch their breath.

'Wow!' He reached out and took hold of her hand.

She was so breathless she couldn't answer.

He squeezed her hand. 'I meant what I said, about making you happy.'

'I know.' She rolled over into his side. 'I'm so tired Callum.'

He smiled and stroked her hair back from her face. 'Get some sleep; we'll talk in the morning.'

'Good idea.' She closed her eyes, cuddling closer, and then she laughed. 'I wonder what Dad will say, when I tell him I'm getting married…?'

Callum sat up slightly on one arm, looking down at her. 'Zoë—'

'He'll have apoplexy,' she murmured, her voice slurred with sleep. 'Especially as he already has his Mr Perfect merchant banker, millionaire friend lined up for me.'

'Is that what he is, a merchant banker?' Callum's voice hardened.

'I don't know what he is.' Through the haze of sleepy exhaustion, she smiled up at him. 'It doesn't matter now, does it?'

'No.' He took a deep breath. 'Maybe your father will just be glad that you're not marrying Matthew.'

'You must be joking. If it's not his idea he won't be pleased.' She closed her eyes and sighed. 'He'll say, ''Zoë, this man I have in mind for you will make a most suitable husband. Trust me on this and at least meet him for dinner. Then you can forget all about this other guy who is filling your head with nonsense.''' She did a passable Irish accent, for a moment reminding Callum forcibly of Francis. 'That's what he said when I led him to believe that I was serious about Matt.'

'Why did you do that?'

'What? Let him think I was in love with Matt?' She grinned. 'Well, it was that or agree to a dinner date with a man I had no interest in meeting. Plus I didn't want Dad to find out about my exhibition. So, pretending I had more serious designs on Matt was a good cover.

'Anyway, I'll ring Dad and break the news to him tomorrow.' Her smile was lopsided now as she cuddled closer in beside him.

'Listen, Zoë...' Callum's voice held an urgent note now '...don't ring him until we've had a chance to talk about this.'

She yawned. 'Don't worry, Callum. He'll come around...eventually.'

'Yes, but we do need to talk before you speak to him.' Silence met his words.

'Zoë?'

There was no answer; she was deep in the oblivion of sleep.

Callum lay back against the pillows and stared up into the darkness of the room.

Who was the man that Francis wanted to introduce her to? He tried to remember his conversation with Francis word for word in case there was some clue he had missed, but the conversation was somewhat hazy now. He remembered him saying something about wanting to settle her down.

Callum grimaced at the memory. He should have had nothing to do with the man's crazy scheme.

He turned to watch Zoë as she slept. A smile curved the softness of her lips; her skin was slightly flushed, her blonde hair tousled on the pillows. But, if he hadn't agreed to Francis's plan, he would never have met Zoë.

When she found out the truth she was going to be furious and he couldn't blame her.

He reached and kissed her lips softly. She responded instinctively, cuddling close to him, enveloping him in the satin, perfumed warmth of her skin. He buried his head against her and tried not to think too deeply about what he had to tell her in the morning.

# CHAPTER ELEVEN

Zoë woke late and stretched in the bed, reaching her hand out to the empty space next to her.

She had heard Callum leaving the room last night. He had pressed a kiss against her cheek. 'Got to go,' he'd whispered. 'The children will be awake soon.'

She had been so exhausted that she hadn't even been able to open her eyes. She'd heard the lock on the door being drawn back and it was the last thing she remembered.

She smiled to herself. Happiness was singing its way through her body. She was so much in love. Callum was the most wonderful, the most handsome and the most caring man in the world. She pulled the covers of the bed back and got out. She'd tell him as well, as soon as she'd showered and got dressed.

She was disappointed when she went downstairs a little while later to find that it wasn't Callum in the kitchen, it was Millie.

'Morning.' Zoë smiled at her brightly. 'How are you?'

'Just fine.' Millie turned and gave her a wide grin.

'Is Callum out working?' Zoë asked.

Millie nodded. 'He said to tell you he'd be back for lunch.'

Zoë made herself some tea and toast. She felt blissfully dreamy. She wondered what Kyle and Alice would say when they heard the news. She hoped they would be pleased. She wanted so much for them to be a happy family.

There was a knock at the front door and Millie went to answer it. 'It was the joiner,' she said when she came back.

'Really?' Zoë grinned. 'I'd given up on him.'

'Well, he's upstairs as we speak.' Millie laughed. 'So keep your fingers crossed that he actually manages to fix that damn window.'

Didn't really matter now, Zoë thought with a smile. The spare room wasn't going to be used again for some considerable time.

She wanted to tell Millie her wonderful news, but contained herself. She couldn't say anything until the children had been told. It would be too awful for them to hear it second hand.

She poured herself another cup of tea and wondered if she should ring her father. Her eyes darted towards the phone in the hall. Maybe later, she decided, losing her nerve. She was too happy to want to spoil things with any negativity.

But she did need to ring Matthew, she thought as she remembered he had called last night. She glanced at her watch and went out into the hall.

He answered almost after the first ring.

'Hi, Zoë, I've been waiting for your call. You're a hard person to catch these days.'

'Sorry. I've just been busy. Is everything all right?' she asked, immediately anxious that there was a difficulty with the exhibition.

'Everything is fine, but I'm looking forward to seeing you next week; there are a few last minute things we need to sort out.'

'No problem. I'll be there.' Excitement shone in her voice. She wondered if Callum could take some time off work and accompany her. She really wanted him at the exhibition. With his moral support, she felt she could conquer the world.

'You sound very happy,' Matthew said.

'Yes...I am.' She took a deep breath and glanced over

at the kitchen door to see if Millie was within earshot. 'I've met someone,' she confided, her voice low. She just had to tell someone.

'Sounds serious.'

'Couldn't be more serious.'

Matt sighed. 'You mean, I've missed my chance.'

She laughed, not for one moment taking that seriously.

'Listen, I saw your dad last week. He called to have a little chat,' Matt continued briskly.

Zoë groaned. 'He didn't give you a hard time did he?'

'No. Actually, he was quite charming. Looked around the gallery and bought a picture.'

'Sounds very suspicious. Are you sure he didn't try to offer you financial rewards for having nothing more to do with me?'

Matt laughed. 'No...more's the pity. He talked a bit about you though. To be honest with you, Zoë, I felt a bit sorry for him. I think he's missing you. Said he hoped that Cumbria was agreeing with you.'

'You told him I was in Cumbria?'

'No. He already knew.'

'How could he know? I haven't told him.' Zoë frowned and then shrugged. 'Doesn't matter, maybe he was speaking to my flatmate.'

She'd really have to contact her father, Zoë thought as she put the phone down. The idea that he might be worried about her and that he missed her pulled at her heartstrings. She was all he had. Could she really blame him for being overprotective? And anyway, she was so happy now she wanted to share that feeling.

She was about to pick up the phone again when the joiner came downstairs and presented her with his bill.

'There's petty cash in the desk in Callum's room,' Millie told her from the kitchen.

'OK, won't be a moment.' Zoë raced upstairs and opened

the drawers of the desk, rifled through the papers and found a wallet.

She was just turning away when a piece of paper with her name on it caught her attention. The writing seemed very familiar. She picked it up to have a closer look.

As she read a feeling of numbness descended, then a feeling of incredulity. Callum knew her father! Callum was doing her father a favour having her here!

Millie shouted something up the stairs, something about not worrying about the money. Zoë couldn't focus on what she was saying; her whole attention was on the letter.

The job here had just been an elaborate hoax. Callum had agreed to it because her father was offering some kind of lucrative contract.

Then she read the line that really blew her mind, 'I know that you really don't want Zoë up there, but if you could use some ingenuity and persuade her to stay for longer than the two weeks, I'd be eternally grateful.'

Zoë could hardly hold the letter steady in her hand as a fierce, raw anger tore through her. Callum had lied to her, deceived her. She found it hard to bear, but it was true.

He'd certainly used some ingenuity to get her to stay. She remembered last night and cringed. Had it all been part of the lie? The passion? The proposal?

She sat down on the bed, her legs feeling too unsteady to hold her. She remembered that his proposal had come just a short time after she had told him she was leaving.

What a fool she had been, what an utter fool. She couldn't believe how completely she had been taken in, or how wrong she had been about Callum.

He had cold-bloodedly seduced her, callously lied to her about his intentions. All he had been interested in was keeping her here so that he could collect a hefty bank balance from her father. Her eyes blurred with tears of pain and she blinked them away furiously.

The man she had thought she was in love with, the man she had imagined was so warm, tender and caring, had been nothing more than a phoney illusion. He wasn't even worth her tears.

'I was going to tell you.' Callum's quiet voice from the other side of the room made her jerk up sharply from the bed.

She stared at him for a moment, frightened that if she spoke she might break down and cry and that would be the ultimate humiliation.

'I'm so sorry, Zoë.' He stood just inside the door, his gaze moving from the letter in her hand to the expression in her eyes.

'You're sorry?' She finally found some strength from somewhere. She was pleased at how angry she sounded, no hint in her voice of the pain and betrayal that ransacked her body, just cold fury dripping through her low tone. 'You bastard…you absolute bastard.'

He flinched. 'Please let me try to explain. I did try to tell you—'

'Oh, yes, you really tried to do the decent thing, didn't you Callum?' She shook the letter like some kind of trophy. 'How much was I worth anyway? How much was dear Papa offering you?'

'It wasn't really like that. Francis was genuinely concerned about you—'

'Oh, please! Next, you'll be nominating yourself for a compassion award. Just being noble were you? Just playing the concerned friend?' She practically spat the words at him, her eyes blazing. 'I trusted you. I believed in you.' For a moment, her voice wavered and she thought she was going to lose control.

'I fell in love with you, Zoë,' he said gently. 'That was never part of the plan.'

She bit down on her lip, pain searing through her. 'Don't

you dare speak about love to me.' She gasped. 'The only thing you loved is whatever incentive my darling father was offering to make you keep me here.'

He took a step forward and she shook her head. 'Keep away from me.' She moved to take a suitcase out from under the bed and then started to throw some clothes into it. She could hardly see what she was doing: her eyes were blurred with tears.

Callum watched her silently for a moment, his hands clenched by his sides as he forced himself not to grab hold of her and physically stop her from going.

'Please listen to me, Zoë,' he said quietly, calmly. 'Yes, I agreed to your father's crazy scheme, yes he offered me a good contract as an incentive. But that wasn't the reason I agreed to do this for him. He was genuinely worried about you, said this guy Devine was a small-time crook and a con artist.'

'Hypocrite!' She flung the word at him violently. 'You're the biggest con artist I've ever had the misfortune to meet.' She had no idea how she was packing, she was just throwing everything into the case. She needed to get away from him as fast as she could. 'What were you going to do? Wait until my father rang and gave you the all clear, then tell me you'd changed your mind about getting married. What would you have said? "Sorry, Zoë, but this isn't going to work. Nice knowing you."'

'No…no, of course not.' He caught hold of her then, his grip tight on her arm as he swung her around to face him. 'I don't want you to go, Zoë…I never want you to go. I've fallen in love with you.'

She looked calmly at the hand that held her, her eyes filled with cold derision. 'You love my father's money, you mean.'

He let go of her then, his eyes hardening. 'I've no interest in your father's money.'

'No?' Her voice shook. 'You're just like all the rest of the vultures that have picked over my life. Out for what you can get for yourself.'

He shook his head. 'That's not true.'

'Stop lying to me Callum. I've just read the truth in black and white. My father offered you a very lucrative contract to keep me here for as long as you could.'

'But I fell in love with you, Zoë. I still want you,' he murmured quietly.

She allowed herself to look at him properly for a moment. He was so handsome, the dark eyes so serious. It tore her heart in two.

'Like hell, you do.' She shook her head and turned away. 'You're good, I'll give you that.' She snapped her case shut. 'I always suspected the other vultures in my life…but you…you had me completely fooled.'

She picked up the case and her handbag and vanity case from beside the bed. 'You can throw the rest of my belongings in the bin.' She turned for the door and found him barring her way.

'Don't leave like this, Zoë. Please calm down and let's talk.'

She took a deep breath. 'There's nothing to talk about.' It took all her strength to meet his gaze steadily and bravely. 'It's over, Callum. Your little ruse is up.'

There was a moment's hesitation. Then he moved out of her way.

She walked past him, her head held high.

'What will I tell the children?'

The question halted her out in the corridor. She stood with her back to him, battling to keep the tears at bay.

'Tell them…' her voice wavered unsteadily '…tell them I love them…but this was only ever a temporary arrangement.'

Then she walked calmly and steadily away from him, down the stairs, out of the front door towards her car. Out of his life.

# CHAPTER TWELVE

THE art gallery was filled with people. Champagne was flowing and people were enthusing about this latest find, this wonderfully talented artist.

Circulating amidst the crowds Zoë heard the flattering comments, saw the red sold markers being put onto the frames of various canvasses, and felt nothing.

This had been her dream for so long, her life's ambition and, now she seemed to have achieved it, it felt worthless. It faded into oblivion next to what she had lost.

Of course, she tried to tell herself that she had lost nothing. How could you lose something when you had never really found it? Yet Callum's dark, good looks and gentle velvet tones continued to disturb both her sleep and her waking hours.

'I fell in love with you, Zoë. That was never part of the plan.' The words haunted her, taunted and tormented her. She'd been back in London for over a week now and she couldn't concentrate on anything. She could hardly eat for thinking about him. And she hardly dared think about the children. Did they miss her? What had Callum told them?

Was Kyle behaving himself at school? Was Callum with Sally?

That question really hit her painfully, low in the abdomen. Perhaps he had lied when he told her he was never serious about Sally. After all, he'd lied to her from the start; one more untruth on top of all the other deceit would hardly bother him. Maybe he'd been serious about the other woman all along and had just played it down to keep her up there until her father paid out.

How could she have been so wrong about somebody?

'Zoë, are you sure you won't sell number twenty-three?' Matt's voice interrupted her thoughts.

'What?' She looked at him blankly, her eyes moving over his blond hair and smooth good looks as if she didn't know who he was.

'Number twenty-three?' he repeated patiently. 'I have a buyer who desperately wants it.'

'Number twenty-three.' She glanced down at her programme. 'Which one is that?'

'It's your final work, the study of the farm in the Lake District.'

'Oh!' Zoë felt her heart going boom, boom, boom, like a mocking parody of a heartbeat in a cartoon. 'No. I don't want to sell that one.' She bit down on her lip. She had finished the study of Callum's farm soon after her return to London. It was the only practical thing she had been able to do, and she had worked on it as if by remote control. She didn't want to sell it...not yet, anyway. It was her one link to Callum and the children.

'I'm sorry.' She shook her head at Matt. 'Tell whoever it is that it's not for sale.'

Matt looked disappointed, but just shrugged. 'Cheer up, Zoë. You're a huge success; this is what you've worked so hard for.'

'I know.' Her voice was flat.

'Have you made things up with your father yet?' Matthew asked in a low tone.

She shook her head. 'I don't know if I'll ever speak to him again.'

'You don't mean that.'

Zoë reached and picked up a glass of champagne from the table beside her. She had phoned her father a couple of days ago and had been furious with him. She couldn't believe how calm he'd been in return. He'd said quite nonchalantly, 'So, you and Callum hit it off, then? I thought you would. That's great, darling. Listen, got to run I'm taking dancing lessons and I'm a bit late.'

Her life was in ruins and he was taking dancing lessons! He got worse, Zoë thought grimly.

Matt's eyes flicked over her. She wore a long red dress that gave her a kind of ethereal beauty. She'd lost a lot of weight recently, and now she had a fragile quality about her, as if at any moment she might break like a china doll. Matt was starting to get seriously worried about her.

'Listen, why don't we go out to dinner after we've finished here?' he suggested suddenly.

She turned to answer and, across the room, her eyes met with Callum's. Shock held her rigid for a moment.

Matt frowned as he noticed her skin grow so pale as to be almost translucent. 'Zoë?'

She looked back at him, her eyes wide and panic-stricken. 'What's he doing here? Matt, I don't want to see him; I don't want to talk to him.'

Matt glanced around and saw a tall good-looking guy in a dark suit shouldering his way through the crowd, a purposeful look about him. 'I think you are going to have to,' he murmured. 'He's the person who wanted to buy that painting of the farm.'

Zoë's lips twisted derisively. She had thought her anger had died, had been doused with sadness. She was surprised to feel it as strong as ever now, rising to her defence. Callum had no right to be here. He was a charlatan, and if he thought he could make things all right between them, and persuade her otherwise by trying to buy that picture, he had another thought coming. 'Matt, put your arm around me,' she murmured, turning pleading eyes on him. 'Help me get rid of him.'

Matt frowned. 'Are you sure, Zoë? Maybe the two of you should talk alone. The room in the back is empty.'

'No!' Zoë took a hasty sip of her champagne and steadied herself. 'Under no circumstances leave me alone with him.'

Matt didn't have time to reply because, as he turned slightly, he found Callum almost by his elbow.

'Hello, Zoë,' Callum said calmly, not taking his eyes from her face. 'Congratulations, the exhibition is wonderful.'

Zoë didn't answer him and, for a second, there was an awkward silence between the three of them, whilst all around the babble of voices seemed loud and intrusive.

'I was just asking Zoë about the painting you were interested in,' Matt interjected. He slipped an arm around Zoë's waist, his manner gentle and reassuring. 'But I'm afraid it's—'

'It's sold,' Zoë cut across him, her voice cool. She didn't want Callum to know she had any sentimental attachment to that canvas.

Distractedly, Callum noticed the arm that the other man had slipped around her waist. His eyes narrowed as they moved back to Zoë's face. 'It's sold? Are you sure? There's no red marker on it.'

She shook her head. 'What are you doing here, Callum?' she asked heavily.

'Unfinished business,' he said, his eyes holding her gaze in a steady, serious way that made her breathing falter, confusing her.

She dragged her eyes away from him, refusing to be drawn into that web of desire and need again. 'I'm busy, Callum, I haven't time for your lies and your deceit.' She finished her champagne. 'Now, if you'll excuse me,' she said with brittle politeness as she put her empty glass down, 'I must circulate; there are friends here, I'd like to speak to.'

Callum reached out and caught hold of her arm as she

made to turn away from him. 'I want to speak to you, Zoë,' he said with determination. His eyes moved to Matt. 'Alone,' he added resolutely.

Matt hesitated. Callum was a good head taller; his senses told him not to argue. He glanced uncertainly at Zoë. Her eyes narrowed warningly. Then he thought about how unhappy she'd been since she had got back. This disconsolate air about her was totally out of character. 'You two need to talk,' he said gently. 'Look, why don't you go into the back room and have some privacy?'

'Matt!' Zoë snapped at him. 'I don't want to—'

'Thanks, mate.' Callum took hold of her arm and practically frogmarched her towards the door Matt had indicated.

'You've got a nerve, Callum Langston.' Zoë rounded on him furiously as soon as he had closed the door behind them and released her. 'I have said everything I want to say to you. Now, get out of my way and let me get on with my life.'

Callum stood in front of the door, his arms folded across his chest. 'Well, maybe you've said everything you want,' he said calmly. 'But I've still got things I want to say to you.'

She tapped her foot impatiently and looked around the room, seeking a means of escape. It was only a small storage room with an office desk. There was one window, but that was too high and too narrow to offer any means of retreat.

'Firstly, I'm sorry.' His voice was deep and serious.

She didn't look at him. 'You've already said that and I don't believe you.'

'Well, whether you believe me or not, it's true. I never set out to hurt you. Your father pleaded with me to help him. I felt sorry for him.'

She didn't reply; she just continued to look away from him, her eyes fixed on nothing, glazed as if she was bored.

'Zoë, he told me he was very sick. Do you realise that he is dying?' Callum's voice lowered to a gentle tone as he tried to tell her this in as sensitive a manner as he could. 'How could I refuse a dying man's request?'

Zoë gave a brittle laugh. 'That old chestnut again.'

'I beg your pardon?' Callum was taken aback. He'd debated long and hard about telling her this. He'd thought she would have been terribly shocked. Instead, she was standing there being harshly derisive.

'There is nothing wrong with my father, Callum. Well, nothing a personality transplant wouldn't help.' For a moment, her lips curved wryly.

'How do you know?'

'Because that's what he always says when he thinks he's not going to get his own way. He's been saying it for years. Did he actually tell you he was dying?'

'Well...' Callum frowned. 'He said he wasn't well—'

Zoë's eyebrows lifted. 'Now, let me guess. What he actually said was, "I haven't got long..."' She supplied the words for him, giving a passable dramatic impression of Francis.

'Yes, that's what he said.'

Zoë shook her head. 'He means he hasn't got long to waste persuading you, so he's going to use the sympathy vote. It works every time for him. He's been pulling that stunt for the last fifteen years.'

Callum looked so stunned that, for a moment, Zoë felt sympathy for him. Her father was a very plausible rogue when he was warmed up on his subject. Then she remembered the letter and the mention of a lucrative contract and she forced herself not to weaken. Only a fool would be taken in a second time, she told herself. Maybe her father had hoodwinked Callum, but Callum's motives hadn't all been altruistic.

'Is that it?' she asked and glanced at her watch.

'No. It's damn well not.' His eyes hardened. 'You're not the only one who's been deceived,' he told her forcefully. 'I was taken in as much as you, by a man I respected and looked up to. I had no reason to doubt the truth of what Francis was saying and I agreed to help on that basis. I know I should have told you the truth sooner but, by the time I realised that things were not exactly the way your father had said, I was in too deep. I was scared of losing you, Zoë.'

Her mouth went dry; she sent a panic-stricken look towards the door behind him. When he started to talk like this, she felt her resolve starting to weaken.

'I love you, Zoë. I love you so much it hurts.' His voice was deep and husky.

She didn't answer him, couldn't answer him. She willed herself not to cry, not to make one move towards him. She told herself that the only reason Callum had said he loved her in the first place was because she had made it clear that was what she wanted to hear.

'And what about Sally?' she asked sardonically. 'Do you love her, too?'

He shook his head. 'I've told you, Zoë. Sally means nothing to me. I've made it perfectly clear to her that my interests lie elsewhere.'

He held her eyes steadily. 'It's you I love, Zoë. After Helen, I never thought I'd say those words to another woman again,' he murmured. 'But I mean them with all my heart. You've lit up my life; you've radiated love and warmth and fun; you've made my life...the children's lives...feel complete again.'

She felt her eyes mist with tears. She wanted to tell him

she loved him, too. But she was scared. Scared of being wrong, scared to trust him again.

'When I asked you to be my wife, I meant it from the bottom of my heart.' His voice was deep and sincere. 'It was the only thing I could think clearly about at the time. I know I should have cleared the air first and told you the truth but I wanted you so much... Getting you to say yes outweighed everything else.'

Looking into his eyes it was hard to doubt him. He was telling the truth. He loved her. She felt the walls of her defences start to crumble. She loved him so much, the thought of life without him was unbearable.

'How...how are the children?' she asked tentatively. 'Who's looking after them?'

'Millie. She's moved in to the spare room until I get back.' He hesitated. 'And, if you want the truth, the children are miserable. They both miss you, but your leaving has hit Kyle especially hard. He's been crying for you.' Callum raked a hand through his hair. 'I haven't known how to tell him you might not be coming back. Hell, Zoë, I don't think I fully realised until that moment how much he misses a mother in his life.'

Zoë bit down on her lip and felt the tears start to overwhelm her eyes.

'I miss you, Zoë,' he said quietly.

She bit down harder on her lip.

'I'll do anything to make this right... I'll sell the farm and move down to London—'

'You can't do that.' She shook her head.

'Why?'

'Because...' she shook her head again helplessly '...because there's no need.'

'If it would make you happy, there's a need.'

'It wouldn't make me happy.'

There was a knock on the door and Matt's voice drifted through. 'Sorry to interrupt, Zoë, but I need you out here.'

Callum stepped to one side and opened the door for her.

She looked at him, taking in the dark eyes, the firm sensual line of his lips. She remembered the taste of him, the feel of him against her skin, the way his arms had held her so gently, so protectively, so passionately.

'I'll be out in a minute, Matt.' She walked over and pushed the door closed again.

For a moment, she stared into Callum's eyes, feeling her heart racing against her chest. 'There's something I want to tell you.'

'What's that?'

'I've decided something.'

'Yes...?' Callum's voice was wary.

'For the first time in years, I'm going to please my father and do what he wants.'

'What's that?'

'I'm going to marry that guy he was so keen to introduce me to.'

Callum's eyes widened. The shock in his expression told her all she needed to know. He had no idea what she was talking about. 'Hell, Zoë, why would you do that? Don't be crazy!' His voice was rough with emotion.

'I'll tell you why.' Zoë stepped closer. 'Because I've damn well fallen in love with him.'

'You've only been back in London a week, how the hell have you managed to fall for some total stranger?'

'Because he's not a total stranger.' Zoë stood in front of him and looked up into his eyes with a smile that was half misted by tears. 'OK, he can be a bit strange at times...and he's a damn Leo...very irritating...but—'

'You can't do this, Zoë,' he said angrily.

'I can,' she said quietly, 'because it's you I'm talking about.'

The confusion in Callum's eyes would have been comical if the situation hadn't been so serious. 'We've both been hoodwinked, Callum,' she explained gently. 'The man my father wanted to introduce me to was you all along. Apparently Dad has had this notion that we would make a good couple. He didn't want to suggest it to you outright because he thought you would baulk against the idea and refuse to meet me…just as I would have. Now, what were Dad's words on the subject…?' She frowned. 'Oh, yes… "I thought the damn man would be every bit as stubborn as you, so I offered a little inducement to get the ball rolling." Quote, unquote.'

'So the whole thing was just an elaborate hoax to get us together… We've both been conned.' Callum sounded dazed.

Zoë nodded her head. 'And he was quite unrepentant when I tore him off a strip—'

'Hold on a minute…did you just say you were willing to go along with all this?' Her words were broken off as Callum suddenly realised what she had been telling him a few minutes ago. 'That you'll marry me?'

She smiled and nodded. 'Maybe it's just easier to give in…seeing as I've fallen in love—'

Before she could finish her sentence Callum had swept her up into his arms and was kissing her.

She kissed him back, her heart and soul in that caress, in the arms that she wound up and around his neck.

When he released her, she was shaking with emotion.

'So, you definitely love this guy enough to spend the rest of your life with him?' Callum asked huskily, looking deep into her eyes.

'No doubt about it,' she whispered. 'I love you, Callum, have done from the moment I first saw you.'

He smiled and stroked her hair back from her face, gazing deeply down at her as if drinking in her features, her smile. Then he kissed her again.

It was a while before they drew apart and, when they did, they were both breathless.

'Hell, I thought I'd lost you, Zoë.' He shook his head. 'And I can't tell you how much that hurt. I'd have done anything to get you back. I kept telling myself, give her time, give her a few days to calm down and she'll understand...but I was afraid you'd never forgive me. It's been pure torture just thinking you wouldn't give me a second chance.'

'I've been pretty tortured myself since finding that letter.'

Callum grimaced. 'But you do forgive me?'

She nodded, and then grinned. 'So, are we going to invite the old rapscallion to the wedding, or what?'

He raised one eyebrow. 'I suppose we'll have to...' he smiled '...seeing as it was all his idea in the first place.'

'Let's discuss the details later,' Zoë murmured huskily, reaching to kiss him again.

# Themed Collections

## Looking for great value and a great read?

**Enjoy Big Savings and Free Books at**
**www.themedcollections.com**

**Western Cowboys**    *Sizzling Suspense*

**Nora Roberts's Classics**

**Debbie Macomber's Latest**

*Forbidden Love*    *Sexy Lovers*

Our editors have handpicked books
from the most popular themes
and bestselling authors to create
fabulous collections—*all at discounted prices.*

Some of our collections are not available
in stores, so come by to check out these
and other compelling collections!

Visit **www.themedcollections.com** today.

THEMAD

# *Harlequin Romance*®

**D**elightful
**A**ffectionate
**R**omantic
**E**motional

**T**ender
**O**riginal

**D**aring
**R**iveting
**E**nchanting
**A**dventurous
**M**oving

*Harlequin Romance*®—
*capturing the world you dream of...*

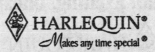

**HARLEQUIN**®
*Makes any time special* ®

Visit us at www.eHarlequin.com

HROMDIR1

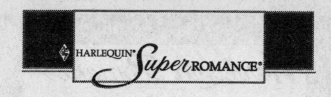

# ...there's more to the story!

**Superromance.**
A *big* satisfying read about unforgettable characters. Each month we offer *six* very different stories that range from family drama to adventure and mystery, from highly emotional stories to romantic comedies—and much more! Stories about people you'll believe in and care about. Stories too compelling to put down....

Our authors are among today's *best* romance writers. You'll find familiar names and talented newcomers. Many of them are award winners— and you'll see why!

If you want the biggest and best in romance fiction, you'll get it from Superromance!

## Emotional, Exciting, Unexpected...

HARLEQUIN®
*Makes any time special* ®

Visit us at www.eHarlequin.com

HSDIR1

# HARLEQUIN *Presents*

**The world's bestselling romance series...**
**The series that brings you your favorite authors,**
**month after month:**

Helen Bianchin...Emma Darcy
Lynne Graham...Penny Jordan
Miranda Lee...Sandra Marton
Anne Mather...Carole Mortimer
Susan Napier...Michelle Reid

**and many more uniquely talented authors!**

Wealthy, powerful, gorgeous men...
Women who have feelings just like your own...
The stories you love, set in exotic, glamorous locations...

# HARLEQUIN *Presents*

**Seduction and passion guaranteed!**

Visit us at www.eHarlequin.com

HPDIR1

# HARLEQUIN®
# INTRIGUE
## WE'LL LEAVE YOU BREATHLESS!

If you've been looking for thrilling tales of
contemporary passion and sensuous love stories
with taut, edge-of-the-seat suspense—then
you'll love Harlequin Intrigue!

Every month, you'll meet four new heroes
who are guaranteed to make your spine tingle
and your pulse pound. With them you'll enter
into the exciting world of Harlequin Intrigue—
where your life is on the line
and so is your heart!

## THAT'S INTRIGUE—
## ROMANTIC SUSPENSE
## AT ITS BEST!

# HARLEQUIN®
*Makes any time special* ®

Visit us at www.eHarlequin.com

INTDIR1

# Harlequin® Historical

From rugged lawmen and
valiant knights to defiant heiresses
and spirited frontierswomen,
Harlequin Historicals will
capture your imagination with
their dramatic scope, passion
and adventure.

Harlequin Historicals...
they're too good to miss!

Visit us at www.eHarlequin.com                HHDIR1

# HARLEQUIN®
*Makes any time special* ®

AMERICAN *Romance*

Upbeat, All-American Romances

HARLEQUIN®
*Duets*™

Romantic Comedy

*Harlequin*® *Historical*

Historical, Romantic Adventure

HARLEQUIN®
INTRIGUE

Romantic Suspense

*Harlequin Romance*®

Capturing the World You Dream Of

HARLEQUIN® *Presents*

Seduction and passion guaranteed

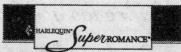

HARLEQUIN® *Super*ROMANCE®

Emotional, Exciting, Unexpected

HARLEQUIN®
*Temptation*

Sassy, Sexy, Seductive!

Visit us at www.eHarlequin.com

HDIR1